WATER GHOSTS

Other novels by Linda Collison
Looking for Redfeather
A Foreword Reviews finalist for YA Indie Book of the Year 2013

Star-Crossed
A New York Public Library Books for the Teen Age 2007

The Patricia MacPherson Nautical Adventure Series:
Barbados Bound
Surgeon's Mate

Nonfiction by Linda Collison and Bob Russell

Colorado Kids: A Statewide Family Outdoor Adventure Guide
Rocky Mountain Wineries: A Travel Guide to the Wayside Vineyards

WATER GHOSTS

A novel

LINDA COLLISON

Old Salt Press

Jersey City, New Jersey

Water Ghosts
Copyright © Linda Collison 2015
Published by Old Salt Press, LLC
ISBN: 9781943404001
ISBN: 1943404003
Library of Congress Control Number: 2015941395
Old Salt Press; Jersey City, New Jersey

Publisher's note: This is a work of fiction. Certain characters and their actions may have been inspired by historical individuals and events. The characters in the novel, however, represent the work of the author's imagination. Any resemblance to actual persons, living or dead, is entirely coincidental.

Under heaven nothing is more soft and yielding than water.

Tao Te Ching

Chapter 1

The doomed ship is set to sail at 10:00 a.m., and I am to be aboard. The taxi has dropped us off at the marina—my mother, her boyfriend, and me. They're here to see me off.

From the parking lot I can see it. *Good Fortune* is unmistakable because it's bigger than the other boats and because it's old and foreign looking. Three masts rise up like pikes from the rectangular deck. A tattered pennant hangs limply from the smallest one. Faded yellow silk.

I don't want to go, but Mother is making me. Walking toward it, carrying my sea bag, I already feel like I'm drowning. Dragging my feet along the rickety wooden pier, past neglected powerboats and sailboats covered with blue plastic tarps, I'm trying to resign myself to my fate. I'm trying to do what Dad used to tell me to do when I was afraid. *Think of something funny!* But nothing funny comes to mind.

Looking around at this run-down dockyard in an industrial park near the Honolulu International Airport, I'm thinking it's wrong, it's all wrong. Hawaii is *not* paradise—at least, not for me. A jet takes off, flying low overhead, drowning us out momentarily with its thunderous roar. Mother covers her ears with her hands and squeezes her eyes shut until it passes. The boyfriend glances at his big gold watch and grins.

"Nine forty," he says. "You'll be boarding soon."

"Oh, James! It looks like an old pirate ship, doesn't it?" Mother's perky voice edges toward hysteria. "A Chinese pirate ship. How cool is that! You are going to have the time of your life. I wish I was going!" She continues to talk, but I can't hear her anymore. Her words are bursts of color, blinding me. I look away.

I see things other people don't see.

The old wooden ship lists in its slip. Doesn't look anything like the picture on the website. Up close the *Good Fortune* doesn't look fortunate at all. It looks bedraggled and unseaworthy, it looks like it's about to sink right here at the dock. I think of a lame cormorant, riding low in the water, awaiting its fate.

Cormorants are different from most other water birds. Cormorants will drown if they don't dry their feathers. That's why you see them on a pier or on shore with their dark dripping wings spread out in the sun and the wind. But they're the bravest of birds because they are not really at home in the water; they're not as buoyant as ducks and geese. They're marginal creatures, living on the edge. They have to work harder to get by.

My father taught me about cormorants. He was a wildlife journalist, specializing in birds. Dad always said he was going to take me on a photo shoot to follow the sandhill crane migration. It was going to be a man-expedition, he promised, an epic father-son trip from Canada to Mexico. We never went.

On the front side of the boat, a painted, peeling eye stares at me. A dead man's stare. An eye that never closes. Is there a matching eye on the other side? I don't want to look. I don't want to know.

"What a piece of junk," I say. "No wonder they call them junks. Can't you see it's a scam? How much did you pay for this, anyway?"

"Don't be ungrateful, James," Mother shoots back. "You're so unappreciative. This is Hawaii. You're starting your summer adventure in Hawaii. How many kids your age get to do that? You are so lucky!" Orange light leaps out from her head, a solar flare. The intense light triggers the song.

With a Yo-Heave-Ho and a fare-you-well
And a sullen plunge
In the sullen swell,
Ten fathoms deep on the road to hell!

I hear things other people don't hear.

The dead men sing as they march through my head, the men from the dream. And now the dream is bringing itself to life in the form of this summer adventure program. Somebody's sick idea of "helping" kids with behavior problems, a sort of boot camp for misfits. Mother found this program on the Internet. Or maybe the program found her, summoned her somehow. She doesn't know she's being influenced by people she has never met, some of them dead.

"What's the matter, James?" Her concern is real. I feel it, little ripples of warmth. But she doesn't get it. At all. Right now we're standing side by side, but we're worlds apart. Like birds and humans, we merely coexist.

I'd like to tell her what the matter is—but what exactly am I going to say? Mother, the dead men are singing. It's a bad sign. The boat is a doomed cormorant that can't dry its wings. That's the kind of talk that gets me into trouble. She hates it when I repeat what they say; she's afraid I'm psychotic or something.

"James?" Gone is the false cheerfulness. Now her aura crackles and spits, a Fourth of July sparkler penetrating my skin with hot little darts.

Mother's face is splotched red from the Honolulu heat. Her once pretty face is now unnaturally fragile, a face stretched too thin, too tight. A face that's known too many Botox injections, too many interventions, a face carefully composed yet beginning to crumble. Yet even now I can see the blue light of her love for me shining through the veil of disappointment. Disappointment and shame.

I look normal enough on the outside (at least, I think I do) but inside me there's this, like, hole—a cavity—that I'm constantly trying to avoid. Sometimes I hear my dead father's voice calling me. *James!* But his voice doesn't come from the hole inside, it comes from behind me, and when I hear it my heart flutters. It's not really him, it's the echoes of his words bouncing around the universe, never at rest. Then comes the weight of his hand on my left shoulder and the sound of him breathing hard, like he's been running to catch up. Sometimes when I close my eyes, I see his face against the backs of my eyes, like a poor-quality video. His lips are moving, but I can't make out what he's trying to tell me.

Mother's boyfriend interrupts my thoughts; his voice is a Doberman's whine.

"He'll be fine. You'll be fine, won't you, kid? Come on, now. Man up!" He reaches out to grip my shoulder, but I step back to avoid it, nearly falling off the dock. I've hated all my mother's boyfriends. I know what it is they want, and it sickens me.

She smiles, her lips tight. "It's just—now that we're here—he seems so young. Compared to the others."

And now I see *them*—three guys sitting on the dock at the end of the pier. They're leaning against new Urban Outfitter gear bags, all sprawled out with their long legs and arms, their hair spiked up with gel. They are cut from the same mold. They could be brothers, they could be triplets.

They're going aboard with me, I realize. We're all in the same boat, we're all going down together. These guys don't seem to know it, or care. They're all holding cell phones, making last minute texts to their friends back home, cigarettes hanging from their mouths. I didn't bring any cigarettes, I don't smoke. But I did bring my lighter. I carry it everywhere because you never know. I brought my cell phone too, but it's already dead, and there's no way to charge it on the boat—that's what it said on the website. I don't know why I even brought it, except the weight of it, deep in the pocket of my shorts, feels solid. Comforting.

My shipmates have man legs, I envy them that. Coarse hair covers their muscular calves like sea grass. Billabong shorts hang low on their hips, they look like some kind of California surf gang. Their feet are all huge in their ragged Converse All Stars: black, brown, red. These three are the shit, and they know it. These fuckers will taunt me, they will make my life miserable—of this I'm sure.

"He'll be fine. He just hasn't got his growth spurt yet. Your boy's old enough. Hell, he's fifteen. Aren't you, Jim? You'll be fine." The Jerk du Jour looks at his watch again. His face is shiny, his Tommy Bahama aloha shirt is all creased and damp, and his gut presses against it like he's pregnant. "It's not like he's going off to war. This is just a cruise, a floating summer camp. They used to send kids like him to military school. Kids these days have all gone soft. Now they get to go sailing the South Pacific. Pretty sweet deal, if you ask me, right Jim?" He has the nerve to wink at me, like we're buds. Like we share a secret. I hate that he calls me Jim.

The truth is I'm here because my mother wants to be rid of me. She can't deal with what I am, with what I'm becoming. She needs me gone. Not like dead gone, just out of sight, out of mind for the summer. So she and the jack-ass boyfriend can—ugh—I can't let myself think about what it is they want to do with each other when I'm not around.

Last summer it was a different boyfriend (I forget his name—I forget all of their names) and the Teens for Christ Summer Camp for me. There I endured six weeks of forced socialization, thrown in with people I had nothing in common with. Of course I was immediately rejected from their group, expelled into the void of oblivion where I remained in orbit around Planet Jesus like a piece of space junk—potentially dangerous but mostly forgotten, a reflected light passing overhead. What were the odds of my reentry? The resident life forms ignored me.

But this summer is going to be worse. Much worse.

⊰⊱

"All hands!" a man bellows through a bullhorn. "Ten minutes till cast off!"

Was that the captain? His voice reverberates through my bones like the crash of a gong, and I nearly piss my pants with fear. This is it. This is where I board the boat, never to be heard from again. Mother bends her head for a kiss. I feel her warm lips brush my left ear as I turn my head away. She touches my shoulder, like she's afraid of me.

"I'll miss you, Jamey honey. Love you!"

I want her to hug me, to be enfolded in those fake-tanned arms. "You don't have to miss me, Mother. You could take me home."

She stiffens and a wave of white light shoots from her head, a scorching flame, a solar flare. She is thinking, *You ungrateful brat!* She's also singed with guilt. I can smell her guilt like a slice of bread stuck in the toaster, smoke filling the kitchen.

"It's not every kid who gets to go sailing on a real Chinese junk for the summer," says the boyfriend, backing her up. Wanting me out of the way. Like he's the one who paid for it. Maybe he was, for all I know. I don't think we have that kind of money.

The energy pulsates from her body, and it's so intense I'm afraid she'll spontaneously combust. Her lips move but the words are drowned out by the dead men from the black hole inside me, chanting that stupid poem again.

> 'Twas a cutlass swipe, or an ounce of lead,
> Or a yawning hole in a battered head—
> And the scuppers glut with a rotting red…
> Yo ho ho and a bottle of rum…

Chapter 2

"What a joke," I croak. I'm talking to the girl who has appeared next to me, a girl who's even shorter than I am. She's an Asian girl who smells like black licorice and is dressed boyishly in a plain white tee shirt, cargo shorts, and sporty water sandals with toe guards like rubber bumpers. Her bitten-off fingernails are painted blue.

We're standing beside the junk of a boat, waiting to be told what to do. The sun is hammering down on us. I'm sweating and my shirt is stuck to my back. The parents have all backed off, retreating down the dock toward the shade the bar offers, fake chummy in that way adults are, flinging easy, empty words at each other. Their voices carry across the water, and beyond—into infinity—colliding with every word ever spoken. It is—what's the word?—cacophony to my ears. Caca and phony for sure.

"This boat doesn't look anything like the photo on the web page, does it?" I say to the licorice girl.

She shakes her head, her fringe of black bangs brush across her forehead. "Heavily photoshopped, I'll bet." Her light shimmers, shades of green and cool, oh, so cool. The same light comes from her hands. Those small, smooth hands.

"I'm James." I flash what I hope is a jaunty smile, holding out my hand, hoping she'll grasp it. She doesn't. Only adults shake hands. I make a fist for her to bump. She ignores it. But she does return my smile.

"Hi, I'm Ming." She's got wide-set Asian eyes and smooth, buttery skin. But she doesn't sound foreign. Close my eyes and she could be the girl next door.

"Ming—that's a pretty name."

She wrinkles her little bump of a nose. "I don't like being named after a dynasty. So impersonal. And the expectations are impossible. But hey, thanks anyway." Her smile is a flash of tiny white teeth. She looks like she's maybe twelve or thirteen, but she says she's fifteen—sixteen in September—from the Upper West Side. Manhattan. I've never been to New York, so I don't really know what that means, the Upper West Side, but it sounds like a movie or a TV show. Way outta my league.

"What did *you* do?"

She looks puzzled. "What did *I* do?"

"To deserve this fate."

She laughs, a buoyant little giggle, and my heart goes ba-Boom. "It looks like a floating prison, doesn't it? Somebody once said that being on a ship is like being in jail—with the chance of being drowned."

"Who said that?"

She shrugs her slender shoulders. Her clavicle bones are exquisite. "I can't remember. Some dead white guy."

"Yeah. Well there are a lot of them. Dead white guys."

She laughs again, a bright burst of sound, but I'm seeing the two of us struggling to get out of a sinking ship, hoping to make the life raft. This vision doesn't come from the dark hole in my mind, this is just a scene from *Titanic*, my mother's all-time favorite movie. *Rose! Rose!* I hear Leonardo DiCaprio shouting over and over as the ship fills with water and the passengers are lowered into life boats, of which there aren't nearly enough. *Ming! Ming!* I'll call out her name as I go down in the icy black water, after having saved her.

She's talking, she's telling me about Suzie, her nanny, who flew with her to Honolulu and is now on her way back to China. I realize I'm staring at the small bumps that break the landscape of her white tee shirt. Plums. Rose buds. *Don't stare!* My eyes fly up to her face.

"A nanny?" I blurt out.

Her face colors, she huffs a sigh. "Yes, a nanny. At my age! Can you believe it? Mostly she just made sure I got to school on time. She cooked me dinner and made sure I did my homework. My parents. They're surgeons. Very busy. Never home. Anyway, Suzie's gone back to China. And I'm not trusted to be on my own. So, here I am." She turns her palms up and shrugs her beautiful bony shoulders.

"Hard to believe our parents could be so gullible," says a boy who has wandered up to join us. He's a squat little guy with big cheeks. He looks uncomfortable and out of place in belted chinos and collared golf shirt.

"Or desperate to be rid of us."

"This is Ming and I'm James." I'm pleased to be introducing her and glad I met her before this little chump did.

The little chump (chump, my dad used that word a lot) is looking at the ship, giving it the once-over. Actually, it's not big enough to be a ship, more like a large boat. As he examines, it his finger drifts up and into his left nostril. He's actually picking his nose right in front of us. Ming and I look at each other. *Oh my God.*

"Now you're supposed to tell us your name," Ming says. "Social cues. You know?"

"Truman," the little dork says in a squeaky voice. He flicks the booger off his finger into the water. "Actually, my name is Wesley, but I hate Wesley. I go by Truman."

"OK, Truman. I'll never ever call you Wesley. Though I might call you True. Where's home?"

He doesn't answer. Truman is staring at the boat, as dismayed as we are. On board, toward the front of the vessel, two old guys are working, tying ropes around barrels. They're wearing baggy, grease-stained pants and worn-thin tee shirts. Dirty bandanas around their heads give them a vaguely piratical look.

"Where do you live, True?" Ming persists.

"Thirty-five-fifteen North Street. New Haven, Connecticut. Zero-six-five-one-one." He's still looking at the peeling gray hulk, the deck of which is cluttered with barrels, crates, and gas cans. His finger wanders up to his nose again.

"Don't do it," says Ming. "Don't pick your nose, Truman. It's disgusting."

"It's a nervous habit," he says, wiping his finger on his chinos. "It's going to be a really long summer. Possibly the longest summer of my life." He glances back toward the tiki bar where the parents are congregated, lifting his arm as if to wave. His stubby fingers flutter briefly before dropping to his side. I think of a bird with a broken wing.

"We'll just have to make the best of it," Ming says, not very convincingly. She swallows hard. Her neck is thin and delicate. Her skin is even toned, without freckles or pimples. Unflawed, like a doll.

"Ahoy!" In the parking lot a woman gets out of a cab. She's waving madly.

"What do you want to bet that's our counselor?" Ming asks. "Miss Marty Bowers. I read about her on the website."

We watch as she comes rushing down to the dock, striped sea bag slung over her shoulder, a clipboard under her arm, and a lei around her neck. Her face is red and glowing. She's a sporty type, like a high school physical education teacher dressed for a regatta, all red, white, and navy blue. Brand new Dockers on her feet. She reeks of coconut sunscreen.

"Roll call!" Her exuberance is unbearable in the face of our despair. "Miss Marty Bowers, camp counselor, that's me. You can call me Miss Marty. Come on, you sailors!" She beckons us with her arm. "Gather 'round now. Step lively!" Shimmering golden light radiates from her solar plexus, and she leaves a trail of sparkles behind her.

The three guys—the big ones—come slouching over. Their bodies have bulk. They have jaw lines, dark fuzz on their upper lips, and a few random hairs on their chins. Bad asses, all bronze and muscular. I hate them already, I hate them defensively. I hate them because I know they'll fuck with me, they will make the last days of my life hell.

Their names are Colton, Myer, and Bastien. It will be hard to tell them apart, except for Bastien, who is a little bigger and taller than the others. His hair is lighter, and his teeth fill his mouth, white and straight as a picket fence. The other two, Colton and Myer, are his minions; they are ready to do his bidding.

And here comes another girl toward us, very reluctantly, dragging her bag behind her. Shiny studs decorate her lips, her nose, her painted eyebrows. The silver sparkles, catches the sun like miniature signaling devices. Says her name's Stephanie, but she goes by Steff. Steff pretty much ignores me, but she's already eyeing the Big Three, and they are aware of her attention. The coal black eyeliner is stark against creamy white skin, and her entire left arm is inked like a colorful sleeve. Don't you have to be at least eighteen to get a tat? Maybe she is eighteen. Maybe it's fake, just painted on. Her aura is dampened, I think she's on something.

The others are already exchanging phone numbers, entering them into their soon-to-be-dead phones. There's no way to charge them on the boat—no electrical outlets, no converters, no generators. Once the batteries go dead or we're out of range, we won't be able to use them anymore.

"OK, you guys, we're about to step onto a time machine here," Miss Marty says, almost giddy with wonder and awe. "The *Good Fortune* is a floating museum, a history lesson, a gateway to the past."

Suddenly my hands turn cold, the black hole widens, the voices mumble and groan.

Looking from face to stony face, Miss Marty tries to engage us. "Are we gonna learn a lot this summer? You betcha! We're gonna learn how to sail and how to navigate. We're gonna learn to work as a team, develop our self-esteem. We're gonna have the time of our lives!"

Ming looks at me with a cocked eyebrow and a knowing, cynical smile. Whispers "Like hell we are," in my ear. Her breath raises bumps on my skin. Goose bumps.

"Who's ready to go aboard?" The counselor's eyes are fairly popping out of her head.

Nobody says a word. We put up a wall, our faces are impenetrable, stone fucking cold. But Miss Marty Bowers is undaunted. One by one she calls our names, her voice a cheerful screech. I'm stealing glances at Ming, her hair shines like a crow's wing in the sun. All I can see of her face is her broad cheeks in profile. The little bump of a nose.

"James McCafferty?"

My head rings with the sound of my own name. I raise my hand and feel the net dropping over me.

"Well then. Looks like we're all present and accounted for." Miss Marty taps her pen against the clipboard.

"Like you need a clipboard," quips Ming under her breath.

There are only seven of us. Seven kids in the country, maybe the whole world, with parents wealthy enough, stupid enough—desperate enough—to fall for this scheme.

"The stupid boat doesn't even have an engine," Ming whispers.

I nod. The website described *Good Fortune* as "an historic Chinese junk, wind driven by canvas sails—an environmentally sound method of propulsion employed successfully for centuries…"

Two guys in a motorized inflatable dinghy are waiting to tow us out of the slip, out of the lagoon, and into the ocean where they will turn us loose. Their little engine idles, putta putta putta, and the smell of gasoline exhaust makes me queasy. I feel like I can't breathe, like I'm already underwater.

Nothing in the world is as soft and yielding as water.

That, from the black hole. But not the dead men chanting. Some new voice.

"Ahoy, Captain Dan! Permission for the crew to come aboard, sir?"

The fat one with the beard grunts and motions us aboard. His face is red as he does something with one of the frayed ropes. "There's a heart attack waiting to happen," I quip to Ming. She snorts.

Miss Marty leads the way. One by one the others pick up their bags and walk across the plank bridging the gap between the dock and the deck. Now only Ming and I are left. The parents are waving from the tiki bar, and I know if I don't get on the boat, Mother will take me home. She'll have to. She can't make me go. Then Ming picks up her bag and starts across. I pick up my bag and follow her aboard.

Chapter 3

We're standing at the stern watching Honolulu sink into the ocean.

"The Pacific Ocean is the largest and deepest ocean on the planet," the counselor says, like she's our tour guide. "And Hawaii is the most isolated population center on earth."

Apparently she doesn't know. None of them do. It's like living among a litter of newborn kittens, blind and helpless. They have no idea.

A gong sounds. We're being summoned for orientation, to "muster," as they call it. We stumble and lurch like zombies across the deck to the appointed gathering place. The ship has become a carnival fun house where the floor buckles and tilts and nothing is as it seems. All we're missing is clowns, scary clowns. Oh, and here they are: our illustrious captain and his first mate. Let the orientation to Hell begin.

First mate, Miles Chu, is the thinner of the two. He doesn't project light, no aura to speak of, and that bothers me. He's the first mate, which means he's second in command. We are supposed to address him as *Mister* Miles, out of respect. At least to his face.

"I'm sure you'll call me all kinds of things behind my back," he says. "But don't let me hear you." I can hear it in his voice, the pleasure he gets from showing off his knowledge, his experience.

"Junks were developed at least two thousand years ago by the Chinese, who not only used their rivers, canals and lakes for transportation, but also set out into the ocean as well." He looks at us sharply to make sure we're paying attention.

"A junk is a beautiful thing. Why? First of all, a junk's hull is built around a series of watertight compartments. The masts of junks are unstayed, and the sails are fully battened lugsails." Now he's losing me. What the hell is he talking about? Does anybody else understand? I want to, I'm listening hard. I'm hanging onto his words like they're life rings, as if words could save me.

"*Good Fortune* is seventy-eight feet long and eighteen feet wide. Her draft is eight feet." I write these numbers in red inside my head so that I can remember them. It might be comforting to recall these facts, to rattle them off like a prayer. But the numbers are meaningless. *Good Fortune* seems really small.

Mr. Miles drones on. "She has the raised stern and the squared-off bow of a traditional Fujian trading junk. So different from your modern sailing yachts and power boats."

"What about the eye?" I blurt out. I'm thinking about the eye on the front of the ship, the staring eye.

The first mate looks annoyed that I've interrupted him, but he takes the time to answer me. "Actually, there is a pair of eyes, one on each side. They are more properly called oculi, plural of oculus. In Chinese, *long mu*. Many ancient cultures painted oculi on their vessels. Understand this, you people: boats aren't just inanimate objects. Boats have souls and the ancient peoples knew this and honored this by painting symbolic eyes."

"What do the markings on the back mean?" I want to know.

"The back? You mean the stern transom," he corrects.

"That's her name, I'll bet," says our cheerful counselor. "*Good Fortune.*"

"Good guess, but no." The first mate smiles behind his impenetrable aviator sunglasses. "Those are auspicious characters, a supplication to the fates. A prayer to Mazu, the sea goddess. Also known as Tianfei. But we'll have plenty of time to talk of Chinese religion and mythology later. Right now I want to finish the tour so you all are familiar with what you need to know." He clears his throat. "The boat has three masts…"

Too much information, I can't take it all in. This much I know: This boat doesn't even have an engine, it's driven by wind power alone. The wind acts on her sails, which aren't white like you'd expect but are the color of dried blood. They aren't triangles either but are shaped more like exotic fans. *Fan* is the Chinese word for sail, which seems a remarkable coincidence.

"The fans are strengthened with bamboo slats called battens," Mr. Miles says. "The battens are the junk's ribs, and they flex in the light breeze as the sails seem to breathe." If the sails are the lungs, then where is the heart? Lungs are no good without a heart.

Mr. Miles wears his graying hair in a ratty little braid. He's got a bald spot on top of his head, revealed when he takes off his bandanna to wipe the sweat from his creased tan neck. He tells us he did four years in the military. He was a Marine. Ooh rah! Semper Fi! But that was years ago, before I was born.

Captain Dan looks more like somebody's fat, stoned uncle than a real captain. He doesn't say much, he lets his sidekick do the talking. Right now Captain Dan stands at the tiller, steering the boat. He pretty much ignores us. He doesn't give off any light either.

"Where's the lifeboat?" I need to see the lifeboat.

Mr. Miles scowls because I've interrupted him again. "Up there. Amidships." He points to a shabby little dinghy turned upside down and lashed to the cabin top. My bowels rumble in fear. This is not a real lifeboat; this is a wooden skiff like you'd rent to go fishing at the state park. There is no way in hell we will all fit inside it. One big wave will crush it.

"That's it? That's our lifeboat?"

"No way that meets Coast Guard regs," says Truman.

The first mate scowls, holding his hand up to silence us. He doesn't say anything more about the lifeboat but instead starts explaining about the tiller and the rudder, how a junk's rudder differs from the rudders of European vessels of the same period. Looking around, everybody's got the same what-the-hell-is-he-talking-about look on their faces.

"In the starboard aft deck locker, we keep the storm anchor, the spare tiller, and the axe. At sea, a vessel must be self-sufficient. We're in our own little world. We need to be prepared for every contingency." Mr. Miles lifts the lid so that we can see inside. The axe alone looks shiny new, fresh from Ace Hardware. It still has a price tag on the handle.

"Now then, let's move forward. Watch your step, people."

The water is rougher, the boat is bumping up and down, and we have to hold onto the railing. Mr. Miles is talking, but the wind snatches his words away. I like the wind, it washes my face, it sweeps my mind of litter.

"...and these are the reserve water barrels where we store rainwater. The lashings must be inspected every watch, got it? Crucial. If these bad boys get washed overboard in a big sea, we're going to get mighty thirsty."

"What's that?" Truman is pointing to a wooden cylinder with rope wrapped around it.

"That's the windlass. The *liao*, in Chinese. A horizontal windlass, used to raise the anchor."

The boat lurches, as if she has tripped, sending Colton stumbling into Miss Marty, who falls against Mr. Miles. Everybody is glad for the chance to laugh, especially me. I'm the last one to stop.

"One hand for yourself and one for the ship," Mr. Miles says, holding onto our counselor a little longer than is necessary. She emits a purple-pinkish glow. "It's a little crowded up here on the foredeck, so take care."

"Yeah. Looks like a redneck's front porch," says Bastien, speaking up for the first time. "All we're missing on this floating shack is a shotgun and a couple of coon dogs."

More laughter. Miles's jaw tightens. He didn't like that crack, but he's cool. "Oh, we have those, in a manner of speaking," he says. "The Chinese carried dogs aboard their *baochuan*. *Baochuan* means treasure ship. They carried just about everything, including hunting dogs."

I see the dogs leaping from the destruction, I see them swimming valiantly, their heads above the water, their legs instinctively paddling, paddling. The dogs won't give up, they will swim and swim until they are exhausted, and then they will go down too. It happened so long ago, but the echoes of their barks, their howls, ring in my head.

"What about guns?" Truman wants to know. "Are we armed? In case of pirates?"

"Most *chuan* weren't built for big guns, they were built for trade. Even the *baochuan* didn't carry the firepower that a British man o' war carried. Conquest was not their mission, you see. They were not expansionists. But the Chinese designed warships in later years, during the Opium Wars…" *Blah, blah, blah.* No one is listening, except for Miss Marty. She is a sponge for his words.

Mr. Miles opens a hatch and leads us down a ladder into one of the many belowdecks storage compartments. This one looks to be about the size of my mother's clothes closet and just as cluttered. Bastien, Colton, and Myer are so tall they have to stoop over. I'm standing on the ladder looking over their shoulders. There's no room for all of us to fit. It's dark down there below the water line and smells like a flooded basement. Something creepy goes scuttling into the shadows.

"Just a centipede," Mr. Miles says.

Peering into the hold, I see what looks like a bunch of lumber and scrap metal—machine parts, twisted pieces of fuselage, the rusted barrel of a howitzer. World War II salvage, we're told.

"Here's a bit of irony," Mr. Miles says. "Did you know that the last sea battle of World War II was fought off the coast of China between three junks?"

Only Truman seems to care about this bit of trivia. He wants to know what kind of guns they carried.

"One was a Japanese junk carrying a seventy-five-millimeter howitzer, and the other two, commandeered by an American Lieutenant, were Chinese fishing junks with only one bazooka rocket launcher between them. Technically, the war was over, Japan had surrendered, but apparently the Japanese thought the other junks were pirates and tried to blow them out of the water. But the Americans and the Chinese fishermen fired a couple of rockets back—with better aim. They took that Japanese junk and that was the end of the naval war in the Pacific."

"Did the Japanese junk sink?" Truman asks.

"No. All three of the junks, though badly damaged, made it back to port. Remember—a junk's hull is compartmentalized. This gives the ship strength and stability. The compartments are watertight, so if the hull is breached and starts taking on water, the leak is contained. So it's harder for a junk to be sunk." He grins at his little rhyme, but nobody else does. Ming twists a shiny strand of hair between her fingers. In my mind I can taste it, her hair between my teeth. Like black Twizzlers.

Mr. Miles goes on. "It was the Chinese, you see, who first used gunpowder in battle. The Song Navy—we're talking twelfth century here—launched gunpowder bombs from catapults at their enemies, the Jin. And this was all aboard ships."

Truman is asking about the howitzer. He wants to know if they can take it on deck and clean it up, restore it, but Mr. Miles shakes his head. "Maybe we'll make a catapult instead and launch some biodegradable trash into the ocean," he says. I have to admit, a catapult does sound like fun.

Now we come to the living area, below deck but above the storage area. Here's the kitchen—the galley—with a propane stove and refrigerator Mr. Miles calls an ice box. Basically, it's just an insulated box, nothing more than a giant cooler for the butter, eggs, and soft drinks.

"Except for fresh fish, all of our meat is canned," he explains. "We don't have to worry about spoilage. We keep the extra stores down in the pantry." He points to a hatch on the deck beneath our feet. "We're pretty much living like people did a hundred years ago, or more."

There's a gong the size of a dinner plate, it's suspended above the sink. It looks like a cymbal. "That's our ship bell," Mr. Miles says. "We use it to announce things, like musters and meals. Strike it with the mallet and watch everybody come running."

Now he's showing us how to light the stove; it's not as easy as just turning a knob or pressing a button. You have to open the valve on the propane tank and the valve on the stove. Then you use a match or a lighter to ignite the gas and then adjust the flame with a knob. There are only two burners and a small oven, not big enough to warm up a pizza. We all take our turn lighting the stove, but I'm looking at the wood carvings on the galley walls. Carvings of phoenixes surrounded by flames, and five-clawed dragons, their twisting, scaly bodies tangled, their eyes colored stones.

"Dragons were good," Mr. Miles says to me, as if reading my mind. "They embodied the yang principle, and they lived either in the clouds or in the waters."

Suddenly the smell of wood smoke is overpowering. I can't get my breath, I'm coughing, gasping. "Fire!" I try to run for the ladder, but someone grabs me by the collar.

"I don't think so," Mr. Miles says, still holding me. "Never say that word aboard a ship, got it? That's no joke, son."

Everyone is staring at me.

"Can't you smell it?" I look at my hands, and they're smudged black, they're covered with ashes and soot. I hold them up to show Ming, but she looks away.

"That's enough clowning around, McCafferty. A fire at sea is nothing to kid about. But don't worry. We have two fire extinguishers on board, per US Coast Guard regulations. One here in the galley and one aft in the captain's cabin." He releases the red cylinder from its holder over the ice box. "Now, in case of a real fire, pull the pin, aim at the base of the flame, squeeze the trigger, and sweep from side to side. Like this." He pretends to pull the pin then makes big sweeping motions.

Can no one else feel it? The fire, the panic, the destruction? Can no one else smell the smoke? Suddenly I am overwhelmed by *his* smell, which I find hard to describe in words, except it's definitely him. My father, alive. Not the burned flesh. I breathe again and it's gone. He's gone. Vanished, just like he did in real life, leaving me with that empty stomach feeling, hungering for something I've never known and can't begin to describe.

"How many of these have you operated, Mr. Miles?" Ming asks.

"What, fire extinguishers?"

"No. Ships like this. With kids like us."

The first mate adjusts his sunglasses. "Hell ships, as they are properly called." His voice cuts, like a broken beer bottle. "Are you asking me for my credentials? Because I've got more sea time than you've been alive."

Everybody is quiet. All you can hear is the water against the hull, a swishing sound.

"There's a chain of command aboard a ship that must be followed. Captain is God: his word is law. First Mate is Jesus: he is second in command. That's all you need to know, understand?"

Ming nods. I see us all on the bottom of the ocean, spending eternity together. We are nothing but heaps of bones, and fish take shelter inside our skulls. I hope my skeleton will be on top of Ming's. I can feel our finger bones, entwined.

"Moving right along, this area adjoining the galley is called the saloon." Mr. Miles extends his arm like a gracious host, indicating the biggest space on the ship. "There won't be any drinking in here, mind you. It's not that kind of saloon." Miss Marty laughs, a tittering sound. A sparrow.

"Saloon is the English word for the officer's mess aboard a merchant vessel. Comes from the French word, *salon*. On *Good Fortune* it's also the crew's quarters. The crew—that would be you people. Your berths are built into the bulkheads, behind those curtains. That's where you sleep, when you aren't on watch. You'll draw straws to see who gets which bunk."

There's a saggy old couch and a dining table where we'll take our meals. Two benches with backs look like church pews. The berths, or bunks, are shelves, one atop the other, stacked three deep, for a total of nine sleeping spaces. Between the berths are bookshelves. There must be hundreds of musty old books.

"That's where we sleep? Looks like a morgue," Myer says, trying for some comic relief.

"Ha!" Miles's voice cracks like a whip. "Yeah it does. After a hard watch on a stormy night, you'll sleep like the dead, I promise you."

"Where do you and Captain Dan sleep?" Steff asks.

"Aft." He jerks his thumb over his shoulder, toward the back of the boat. He tells us the smaller cabin on the port side is his cabin. The other one, the thick door with the five-clawed dragon carved into it, is Captain Dan's quarters. He goes on to say that these stern cabins are strictly private, off-limits to us. The doors remain shut; we don't even get to look inside.

"Moving on, this here is the nav station. Navigation is a super important skill for any mariner to master." Mr. Miles redirects our attention to a desktop at the aft end of the saloon, a surface piled high with books, manuals, and charts. "This is where we keep the official ship log and the working chart." A map of the Pacific Ocean, creased and stained, is folded in quarters with little pencil marks all over it. Hanging above the desk is another carving, some demonic-looking god. His stone eyes are missing. He looks blind, and his body has been charred black from the fire. But I don't say anything. I concentrate on breathing slow and deep so I don't panic. *Stop making things up, James.* Mother's voice rings in my ears. *You're scaring me.*

"You'll learn how to read a chart, and how to plot a course using simple tools. And this here is the shortwave radio." Mr. Miles pats an archaic-looking black box, half-hidden in the clutter. "Worst case scenario, if the ship is going down and you need to call a Mayday, first make sure the radio is hooked up to the battery and the power button is on. Then key the mike and say Mayday, Mayday, Mayday. Then identify yourself. 'This is the sailing vessel *Good Fortune*.' Repeat it. Give your last known position, which you know from the chart or the logbook. State the nature of your emergency. It must be a life or death situation—you don't call a Mayday just because you've run out of rum."

A nervous burst of laughter from all of us. Even me.

"Something else you should know: these flares." The first mate holds up three red cylinders. They look like bottle rockets. "You launch a flare only when you can see the rescue ship or aircraft approaching. Don't want to waste them." He puts the flares back in the box and turns on the radio, turning the dial. It makes weird noises and then lapses into silence. Dead. Mr. Miles turns it off. "Don't want to run down the battery."

"That's an old crystal radio, with vacuum tubes and shit," Truman whispers to me. Fucking ancient!"

"Real sailors don't depend on fucking electronics," the first mate quips. "Ancient or modern." Obviously he can read lips or has superpower hearing. "Magellan, Cook, and Zheng He, they all sailed the world without them. What, you don't know Zheng He? Well, you will. I promise. Zheng He didn't need no stinking electronics." His lips twist up in a contrived smile. "Any questions?"

Ming raises her hand. "The website said this boat has been inspected by the Coast Guard and has everything we need aboard for our safety."

"I didn't write the website. But I can assure you we have everything the Coast Guard requires us to have. We are a documented vessel. We have a type one PFD for every person aboard. We have an assortment of pyrotechnic visual distress signals, including a couple of aerial red meteors and launchers, which, by the way, should only be used when the rescue vessel or aircraft is in sight." He's ticking these items off on his fingers. "We have two approved fire extinguishers. We use lanterns for our navigation lights. And we have an approved sound producing device, that is, a foghorn and a bell, as required. Satisfied? Because the US Coast Guard is satisfied. But when you go to sea, you have to be self-reliant. It's a big ocean out there, boys and girls. You can't go expecting someone to come save your sorry ass when you get into a situation. No matter how many modern conveniences you have, when the shit hits the fan, you can't count on any of them. Not really. You know what you can count on? Murphy's Law."

"So, no GPS." Truman can't hide his disappointment. His face droops, the shine goes out of his eyes.

Mr. Miles pats his front pocket. "I'll let you in on a little secret. I've got a hand-held unit I keep on my person at all times, strictly a backup. But we won't be depending on it. We're navigating the way our ancestors did. The Chinese and the Arabs sailed the seas with only a compass and a star chart. Hell, the Polynesians populated the Pacific and they didn't even have a compass. How did they do it?" He taps his forehead. "They carried their maps up here. Star maps, people."

Group thought: *This is not what our parents paid for. This is the twenty-first century. We are US citizens, our parents pay taxes, and we have certain unalienable rights.*

Mr. Miles removes his shades and looks from face to face as he speaks. His eyes are as deep as the ocean, the universe. "Folks, this ain't no harbor cruise. This is the real deal. You guys are all on board because your parents think, or maybe the judge thinks, you need a reality check, some hard work and discipline, a life-altering experience. Well, this is it, baby. This is your life-altering experience. And it can be challenging. It can be character-building. It can even be fun. Or it can be a floating hell. You choose."

Chapter 4

We're all at the stern of the boat watching Captain Dan steer. Mr. Miles is doing the talking. He's explaining how the tiller, the *duo bing*, moves the rudder, the *duo*, and how it's the force of the water moving against the rudder that turns the *chuan*, the general word for boat. The *duo* is cut with diamond-shaped holes, making it easier to maneuver.

"Early Chinese *duos* differed from early European rudders. Chinese rudders were more adaptable. They could be raised and lowered. The *duo* gives the junk greater stability in deep ocean waters."

None of this means anything to me, it's all way over my head. I'm staring at Captain Dan's fat hand. Looking at the gray hairs on his knuckles. Who has hair on their fingers?

We draw straws to divide ourselves into three watches. Truman and Myer are the red dragons; Ming, Steff and Colton the yellow dragons; and Bastien and I, the blue dragons. None of us are happy with the arrangements, least of all me. Even Colton, who's lucky enough to be paired with both girls, is already having anxiety separation from Bastien. Colton is Bastien's bitch. He would do anything for him.

I'm just hoping to survive the next two weeks when we'll choose new watches. Truman says there's one chance in thirty-five that the three of us—me, Ming, and Truman—will be on the same watch. The odds improve to one in six for me being on watch alone with Ming. But I don't get my hopes up. I'm not what you'd call a lucky boy. The gods who rule my life are all petty and spiteful. If they think I want something to happen, they take pleasure making sure it doesn't.

"Listen up, crew. Tomorrow morning, and every morning hereafter, you'll find your day's work posted on the cork board at the nav station."

Galley duty, housekeeping, ship maintenance, lessons, safety drills, and group sharing sessions with Miss Marty will consume our mornings and afternoons. In our free time, which is precious little, we have to do our ablutions, which means personal hygiene. We have to wash our clothes at the laundry station—which is two tubs of water—on deck. We have to wash them like they did back in the day, with a bar of soap and a washboard. There's a line strung between the masts to hang them on. The hours to be endured, the days to survive, tower over me. I wish I had wings. I wish I could teleport myself back to land.

Starting tonight, from eight until eight in the morning, we'll take turns standing watch. The watches are to be measured the old Chinese way, by burning an incense stick. When it's our turn to be on deck, we have to keep the boat on course, he says. It's our responsibility. And we have to keep a lookout.

"For what?" Ming asks. "What exactly are we looking out for?"

"Anything out of the ordinary," Mr. Miles says. "A change in the weather. Other vessels we might be in danger of colliding with. Floating debris, like containers that fall off of barges. Or maybe an uncharted reef that might wreck us if we don't steer clear." He adjusts his shades, for emphasis. He lifts them a little and sets them back on the bridge of his nose. "This isn't high school, people. Aboard this vessel we all depend on each other for our very lives."

Bastien is pretending to be bored. His arms are folded across his chest, his eyes are half closed. But I hear his heart thumping. I know it's his heart. And a sick yellow light oozes from his skin.

⌘

Lunch sticks in my throat. I have no appetite for the juice boxes, the premade ham and cheese sandwiches wrapped in cellophane, the canned peaches. The rolling and swaying of the boat is churning my stomach, my brain. I'm not the only one. It cheers me a little to see Bastien at the rail, spewing his lunch. There's a word for that, taking pleasure in the misfortune of others. I can't remember it, don't really care. I don't want to throw up. I will myself not to get sick.

Ming feels absolutely fine. She eats her lunch and half of mine. Turns out she's wearing a timed-release medication patch behind her left ear to prevent motion sickness. Scopolamine. She turns her head and pulls back her hair, like she's sharing a secret. There, a little flesh-colored circle stuck to the skin behind the petal of her ear.

"I'll give you one of mine, James. I brought extra, just in case." She reaches into the pocket of her shorts and brings out a Ziploc bag of magic patches. "They're prescription. You aren't allergic to any medicine, are you?" She pauses, the potent dot balanced on her fingertip.

"Nah." I hold my breath as she touches my chin and turns my head so she can see my ear. When I feel the pressure of her finger against my skull, I forget my nausea. She touches me and I'm cured. For a few minutes I forget that we're all about to die.

⧉

Man overboard! That's what you shout out if somebody falls off the boat. We're having our first drill. Miles throws an empty cardboard box off the side and tells us that's Miss Marty and we are to save her. She waves her arms, jumps up and down on the deck, and cries "Save me! Save me!" And even though it's only a drill, I feel a surge of fear. We all do as we stumble around the deck like a bunch of clumsy clowns, each fumbling to do our assigned task. Steff keeps her eye on the man overboard. She stands at the rail, pointing. Colton throws the life ring and notes the compass course. Ming puts the tiller all the way over, and the rest of us work the sails to get the junk going in the opposite direction. When we finally get the junk jibed around and head back to retrieve the box, we've lost sight of it. Maybe it's already sunk.

"If that had been your counselor, she'd be a goner. Now you see why we need to practice these things. But an ounce of prevention is what will save your life. Because the reality is this: People who fall overboard are shark bait. It's a sad fact. The ocean swells swallow them up. They might be fifty feet away, but if they're in a trough you won't see them. Especially at night. They stay alive until they drown from exhaustion, hyperthermia, or along comes a tiger shark and takes a bite out of them and they bleed to death. So the real lesson is, don't fall in, mates." Again, the twisted little smile.

There's a sick silence onboard. All I can hear is the restless murmuring of water against the hull as we plough through the waves.

"Oh, and gentlemen—resist the urge to relieve yourselves over the side. Especially in rough seas. Use the head or use the bucket kept on deck for just that purpose. The bodies of men who have been recovered all have one thing in common." He pauses for effect. "Their flies are unzipped. Don't let it happen to you."

Now the boys laugh and I join in. Har har har. Yuk yuk yuk. The sound of dogs barking.

"Looks like we need a little more practice at the tiller and reading the compass. Come on, let's have at it."

The compass is mounted on a box called a binnacle, a *zhen fang*, where the person steering the boat can easily see it. Around the needle are two cards. The inner circle has the cardinal directions north, south, east, and west. Each quarter is further divided into one hundred and eighty degrees. N is 0 degrees, E is 90, S is 180 and W is 270. The inner circle is divided into forty-eight sections, each one illustrated with a tiny Chinese character painted in gold. We each take a turn at the tiller, the *duo bing*, a long wooden pole, kind of like an oar handle, worn smooth from so many hands gripping it. I have a fear of touching it, of taking hold. What if my sweating hand summons some long-ago helmsman?

Now it's my turn, I take a grip. Through it I feel the might of the ocean against the rudder. I feel the force of the water and the wind transmitted through the wood to my arm, my whole body. I've never known such power. I'm amazed they trust me to do this.

The ship rocks us roughly, like a resentful mother. The sunlight bouncing off the surface of the water feels like needles in my eyes. Miss Marty hounds us to drink more water, to put on more sunscreen, to wear hats, blah, blah, blah. She's a continuous public service announcement. But who wants to drink warm water? Who wants another juice box? I crave an icy cold Mountain Dew.

"Half an hour of free time, you lucky sailors," Miss Marty says. "It's my turn at the tiller. The first mate is going to give the counselor a lesson in helmsmanship. Now would be a good time to start getting to know one another." She has braided her hair into a short club, she wears a thick stripe of zinc oxide on her nose, like toothpaste. I can feel her giddy attraction for Mr. Miles, it feels like the first swallow of that Mountain Dew I'm dying for, a rush of sweet, stinging fizz. Effervescence. Like what I feel when I look at Ming. My hand goes behind my left ear where she touched me. The patch is still there, delivering its magic into my bloodstream.

At first we're reluctant to talk about ourselves. We make offhand comments, trying to sound older than we are. But we're messed up, all of us, of that I'm sure. This program was designed for us—kids with behavior problems. Gradually it begins to come out, the problems in school. Colton and Myer, they're both on medication for ADHD. Steff was hooked on pharmaceuticals, her grandmother's Oxycontin.

Me, I haven't been diagnosed with anything. My mother is afraid to take me to the doctor, I haven't even had all of my immunizations. But it's not measles or diphtheria she's afraid of.

"I'm here on court order," Bastien brags. "It was this piece a shit boat or juvie hall for me."

"What'd you do?" Steff is clearly impressed.

"Nothin' really. Kicked a little ass. Busted some face."

"Why?"

He shrugs and smirks. "I didn't like his ass or his face."

Colton and Myer look to him for permission to laugh, which he grants with a nod. Yukka yukka yuk.

Truman and Ming haven't revealed anything, and neither have I. The others ignore us.

⊲⊳

Eight o'clock. It's been an exhausting first day, and now the first night stretches before us. Bastien and I will stand watch from midnight to four in the morning. "Better turn in," Miss Marty advises. Dressed in pajamas festooned with blue anchors, she crawls into her own bed. "Get some sleep while you can." Our counselor extinguishes all of the lanterns except one, in the adjoining galley, over the stove. She lowers the wick on that one until it burns feebly, like a night light.

To get into my berth I have to stand on the edge of Bastien's bed and hoist myself up. As I do he grabs both my ankles, and I come crashing down, landing on my ass.

"You fucker!" Me, yelling.

He pulls his curtain shut and fake snores.

"Boys!" Miss Marty calls out. "No horsing around. You need your sleep."

This time I climb up really fast, before he can dick with me again. Quick, pull the curtain closed. The curtain is a piece of old sailcloth, water stained and sticky with salt. Now here I am, alone at last, tucked into my own little morgue shelf. It feels like a safe haven, at least until we go down.

Secluded behind the curtain, I reach for my few belongings to reassure myself. My oversized gym bag, which contains my toilet kit, three changes of clothes, sweat pants, a hoodie, and a water repellent windbreaker, all intact. In the deep side pockets of my cargo shorts, I feel my father's cigarette lighter and my cell phone. My useless cell phone. This morning it was fully charged and now it's dead. Those greedy little bastards, the ones who chant in my head, are always sucking the power from my electronics. I slide my thumbs over the dark screen, like I'm texting a message, and then I hold it against my heart to send. Putting that back, I fondle the butane lighter that was my father's. Engraved with his initials. My initials.

My little ritual is complete—except I forgot to brush my teeth. I'm not going to do it now, I don't want to get out of bed and have Bastien mess with me again. Fully clothed, I nestle into my sleeping bag, curling into fetal position. Breathe in the warm dampness of my own body, the smell of sweat and fear. My hand slips down into my shorts to hold myself. Tenderly, for reassurance. The boat rocks me, rocks me, rocks me to sleep.

⊣⊫

"You're up, James. Your turn for watch."

Doodley-doo. Ming's clarinet voice wakes me, a soft stirring in my ear. She is leaning close to me, and her hair brushes my cheek. For a second I'm disoriented, then I remember. It must be midnight. Me and Bastien are on watch for the next four hours.

I slide from my bunk, my stomach in knots. I'm dreading this, I don't want to be on watch. What if I screw up?

Out on deck it's a different world. The black velvet sky is littered with stars. Who would have thought there could be so many? Starlight on the ocean, ripples of liquid mercury—it's thrilling, really, but colder than I would have thought. We're somewhere south of Hawaii, and I'm shivering inside my windbreaker and long pants. Ming hands me a fresh incense stick, and I reach into my pocket for the lighter. The incense sticks are designed to burn slowly, to mark the passage of a four-hour watch. I light it and place it in the holder, a tin sconce attached to the *zhen fang*, the box-like thing that also holds the compass. The course is 120 degrees, southeast; it's written on a scrap of paper and taped to the *zhen fang* so we don't forget.

"G'night," says Ming, and goes below. "I'll try again to wake up Bastien."

"Here, take this stupid thing," Colton says. Reluctantly I take the tiller, the smooth wooden pole that steers the ship. Colton goes to the rail and takes a stance, his back to me. He's a shadow, a silhouette, a figure cut out of black construction paper with his legs spread slightly. I can't see his hands, but I know where they are. The swells are big, muscular, pushing the beam of the boat like a schoolyard bully. The tiller wants to jerk out of my hand. I'm worried Colton's going to fall overboard, the stupid ass. He's not holding on, he's pissing like a real man.

"Better use the bathroom. The marine head," I say. "Remember what Miles said. About falling overboard."

Colton turns and aims his stream at me and I duck, but not quickly enough. "Piss on you, Jimmie." He laughs, shaking his thing like a rope. Then he disappears, going below deck to turn in.

And now I'm alone up here, I'm steering the ship all by myself. I'm actually *steering* the ship, and it's dark, and there's nobody on deck but me. Everybody is depending on me to steer the ship. The compass needle is swinging in arcs. I'm trying to bring it back to 120, but it swings too far the other way. No! I jerk the tiller back, there's a pause, and the needle comes flying over, but again too far. Now the booms swing and the sails lose their air, something doesn't feel right. I forget where the needle is supposed to be pointing. My mind freezes up, I have no idea what I'm supposed to be doing. And now I know that this is how the premonition comes true, I'll sink the ship by my own hand! It will be my fault, like it always is. I wish I could hear my father's voice, telling me what to do. And then I do hear a voice, but it's not my father's. It's a thundering bellow. It's Captain Dan.

"What the hell is going on up here?"

My throat's so tight I can't answer, I can hardly breathe. The captain takes hold of the tiller, his big warm hand just behind mine. He reeks of alcohol. His hair is a fright, his beard blowing in the wind. He looks like some crazed old prophet. Thank God! Relieved, I gladly let go but he says, "Wait—keep your hand on the tiller. Feel what I'm doing. You're making it too hard." His voice is gentler now, the edges of the words blurred and smeared together. Maybe he's not a zombie or an evil ghost. Maybe he's just an old man who's had a little too much to drink. But he's not afraid, he knows how to sail this ship. Maybe we're not going to sink after all—at least, not tonight.

"Relax, kiddo. Don't fight the ship. Steady, steady, steady she goes. That's it. Don't stare at the compass. Close your eyes, feel the wind against your face. Steer by the wind."

I close my eyes and feel the cool damp air against my left ear.

"Feel that?"

I do. And I feel safe, for the first time in days. Maybe years. I feel the wind steady on my cheek, and I want this feeling to last forever.

We're back on course, I can breathe now. Everything is OK. The captain lets go of the tiller. I'm steering on my own.

"Where's your watch mate?" Captain Dan asks.

"Who?"

"Where's the kid who is supposed to be standing watch with you?"

I shrug. "Maybe he's in the bathroom. I mean, the head." I know where Bastien is—down below, asleep in his bunk. But I don't say that. I'm not going to bait him out. I've never been a snitch.

"That's OK. I'll find out soon enough. There'll be no shirking of duty on this boat." The captain leaves me at the helm and strides to the companionway, his feet heavy on the deck. From below I hear a curse and a yowl like a cat whose tail is being yanked. Suddenly Bastien appears, stumbling to the cockpit bench, still in his bare feet.

"You two have the helm," Captain Dan says, sticking his head up to peer out of the companionway. "Call me if you need me. Don't over correct, McCafferty. Steady as she goes. Should be an easy night."

A long minute passes. We hear his cabin door open and close.

"Crazy old fuck," Bastien mumbles.

"We're supposed to do a deck check at the beginning of the watch," I say. "You want to do it?"

"Hell, no. I'm not moving from this bench, got it? You want to go wandering around in the dark on this leaky old tub, be my guest." Zipping up his hoodie, Bastien curls up on the bench, his crooked arm for a pillow.

The captain's coming. I hear his footsteps, the vibration through the deck. Bastien hears too and jumps to his feet, yanking the tiller away from me.

"I'll steer the boat. You go check the deck," he orders.

And I obey, hating myself. Creeping forward on the windward side of the boat, holding onto the rail with a death grip. The boat rises and then falls beneath my feet as I make my way along the deck, gripping the edge of the bulwark, slowly, awkwardly. I feel like a toddler just learning to walk. Now

I've reached the cluttered foredeck, but I've forgotten what it was I'm supposed to inspect. Lashings? Lines? Water barrels?

We're supposed to keep a lookout too. *That* I remember, but looking out over the open bow, I don't see anything but darkness. The boat rises up to meet a dark hill of water and cracks it in half, drenching me with cold water. For a second I can't breathe, I've had the wind knocked out of me. I'm dripping, shivering, and when I catch my breath, I start laughing. I can't help it. I'm laughing out loud, and I don't know why because I'm terrified. The black hole inside me is now all around me, the only thing keeping me from falling into oblivion is *Good Fortune.*

"What are you laughing at, you demented little freak?" Bastien calls out. "Get back here!"

He's afraid, I can hear it in his voice. I can feel his anxiety like the icy wave breaking on my back. Bastien is afraid. We have that in common. Our fear makes us equals and I'm glad for that.

Chapter 5

We're supposed to be writing in our journals. "Journaling," Miss Marty calls it. How that is different than writing I haven't figured out yet. The good thing is she doesn't care about grammar or handwriting or grading us, but thirty minutes after lunch is allotted for journaling so that's what we're doing. We're sitting in the shade of the sails pretending to write in our notebooks while Miss Marty keeps track of the creeping minutes with a sandglass, like the one the witch uses in the Wizard of Oz to mark the minutes remaining in Dorothy's life.

But we don't journal. Instead, we goof off, we show off, we write stupid, hateful things and then snatch each other's books away and read them aloud. It's turned into a contest of who can be the funniest or the dirtiest. No one admits to anything real.

Except Steff. She's trying to describe a dream she had last night. The words don't come, so she sketches a picture. Bastien snatches her notebook away and holds it up for all of us to see.

She draws really well. Except—my heart bumps—she's drawn *me*. Only my head is severed from my body and rests on my hands, like I'm carrying a precious vase. Tears drip from my eyes and blood spouts from my neck. I am a martyr; I am St. James of the Apostles.

"Give me that!" Steff grabs it back, both pleased and embarrassed at the attention. Her vampire-white cheeks stain pink, and I catch a whiff of her dream.

"We're entering the Pacific portal," I say, the words flying out of my mouth like a sneeze, nothing I can do to stop them. "It's a gateway, a wormhole for these spirits to pass through, but sometimes they get caught—"

"Shut up, you little nutter," Bastien says, "or I'll turn your asshole into a wormhole."

Colton and Myer go yukka yukka yukka. I do it too, I imitate their laugh. I'm mocking them. I'm laughing and Bastien reaches over and smacks the back of my head. Playfully but hard. I shove him back. He gets me in a choke hold.

"Leave him alone, Bastien," says Ming.

"Yeah. Let him talk. Maybe he's clairvoyant or something," says Steff. "Hey James, can you interpret my dream? Can you predict the future?"

I can't. The voices are unpredictable. They've gone silent, back down in their hole. I have to make something up. The girls are looking at me, waiting for me to say something.

"Captain Dan and Mr. Miles are possessed," I say. "They're, like, zombies. Undead. And they've been sailing this junk around for, I don't know, decades. I think they want to turn us into zombies too." Now they're all listening. Even Bastien. It feels good to be the center of their attention.

"Think about it. They almost never take their shades off. Have you ever looked into their eyes?"

I'm making this up as I go, I'm flying by the seat of my pants. Captain Dan and Miles probably aren't evil. In some ways they remind me of my father. Lost boys inhabiting the bodies of old men like hermit crabs taking over vacant shells and empty cans of tobacco. But everybody is waiting to hear more. Even Bastien. So I tell them something I do believe. That we're all here for a reason. That some power has brought us together on this junk. That it wasn't random chance.

"I think we've each been chosen. Handpicked."

"By who?"

"And why?"

"I don't know. But somebody wants us. Somebody or something wants us very much."

And then my moment is over. Miss Marty comes up on deck carrying a crate of empty liquor bottles like a treasure chest: Captain Morgan, Jack Daniels, Cuervo Gold. She has an assignment for us.

"OK, guys, here's what we're going to do." She presses her palms together like she's praying and looks from face to sullen face. "We're going to write a letter, each one of us, to someone important in our lives. We're going to tell them how we really feel, and we're going to be open and honest. Then we're going to roll up the letter, put it in the bottle, and seal it."

We're looking at her with blank faces. Our masks protect us. At home we would never do such a thing, but there is something comforting about putting a heartfelt message into a bottle and launching it into the ocean, the graveyard of so many human aspirations.

"Maybe you're angry with someone, or maybe someone in your life has let you down. Or maybe you've let someone down, someone you care about. Let's say you've hurt someone and want to say you're sorry. Make amends. Ask forgiveness. Redeem yourself. That's what this exercise is all about." Miss Marty's round face radiates empathy, which I soak up. I am a sickly little sapling pushing through the snow, eager for her sunshine.

"What if we're not sorry?" asks Ming.

Miss Marty's smile just grows bigger, her plump cheeks pushed to the max. Nothing fazes her. She's a beacon of hope. "Then just ask for what you need. Acceptance? Love? Put your true thoughts and feelings onto paper and into the bottle. Put your desires out there to the all-powerful universe."

"My desire is to be stinking rich," says Bastien. "I wanna be a billionaire so fucking bad," he sings, imitating Travie McCoy's voice to the T. Everybody laughs, even Miss Marty. She never seems to get angry, she is unflappable.

While the others are arguing over who gets which booze bottle, I'm already writing in my notebook. Writing to my father is easy. The words run out through my fingers like water, I don't even have to stop and think about what I want to say. He's more alive to me than my mother is. It's my mother who's the ghost, wanting to be alive but not quite knowing how.

The weird thing is Dad doesn't seem to realize he's dead; he hangs around like he's still one of us, like nothing happened. He doesn't notice his flesh is starting to fall off his face, he doesn't pay any mind to his charred hands. I hear his voice every so often, calling to me. *Hey James, wait!* I hear him panting to catch up. *Hey, big guy, wanna hang out, or are you too grown up to spend time with your old man? I got us some tickets. What say we catch the afternoon game?* I hear the slam of his car door, I hear his footsteps on the pavement, I smell him as he approaches. He wants to spend time with me.

The funny thing is my dad never said any of that when he was alive.

⊣⊟⊢

My parents split up when I was three, so I don't remember them together. I can't even imagine them under the same roof, they're from totally different planets. My mother always refers to him as "your father." She can't bring herself to say his name.

Jack. Jack McCafferty. Just by saying it I can summon him, conjure him up, and he is so ready to make amends, to be the father he never was in life. He's kind of like a dog, anxious to please, and he comes whenever I call him. And I reinvent him, Jack McCafferty, aka Dad, over and over. He's bigger now, in death. Kinder. More fun to be with. And happier. He doesn't need the junk anymore, and he doesn't need to drink. He no longer smells like old cigarettes. He is my perfect father.

Hey, Dad. Miss you. Wish you were here, but maybe you are afraid of water too? I don't blame you. But water covers fire, it obliterates it. Guess I deserve this fate, huh? Please forgive me. I wish we could just start over.

I choose a Hana Bay rum bottle. *Yo ho ho.* Tear out the sheet of paper with the message on it, roll it up tight like a joint, and stick it inside. Put the cork in. One by one we chuck our bottles over the side. They bob in our wake, like a family of glass ducklings, green and brown.

"I wish I had an AK-47," says Truman. "It would be fun to shoot them."

Truman has a thing for weapons. That's why he's here, because he bought an assault rifle, online. His parents found it under his bed with a bunch of back issues of *Guns & Ammo* and *Shooting Times*. They totally freaked. Thought he was planning to go shoot up his classroom—which he swears he wasn't. He just wanted to possess it, to hold it, to take it apart and see how it works. Which I kind of understand. I mean, I know what it's like to find comfort in something so powerful. Something that can level the playing field.

Chapter 6

W e're getting to know one another, we're forming our little alliances. I'm kind of stuck with Truman, but I don't mind. He's the youngest of us. He just turned fourteen two weeks ago, but he still picks his nose like a two-year-old. Without shame. I'm guessing he's Asperger's. A lot of kids are Asperger's these days, it's a popular diagnosis. Nobody really knows much about it, but it might be nice to have a medical name to explain your behavior.

The Asperger's kids I know are kind of quiet, except when they're really excited about something. Some of them are really smart, which Truman kind of is. His main obsession is guns, and he knows a lot about them. Makes, model numbers, calibers. He collects facts, stores them in his head, and rattles them off like the rosary. I think it's just his way of feeling OK, of keeping the anxiety in check.

But it's not Truman and his assault rifle I fear. I see an axe being dragged along the deck. I can't see who's dragging it, but I see the person's bare feet, small, like a child's. I smell the axe, the rusty metal edge, or is it blood I smell? I can't breathe. I'm choking on my own blood, blood bubbles from my mouth.

"Dude, you OK?" Truman looks at me, actually makes eye contact for the first time. A little shadow crosses his face. He's not sure what he should do.

The hallucination is gone, it leaves a filmy residue inside my head. I feel like I'm going to puke. "I'm fine, thanks. Just feeling a little sick." I force a fake smile, which fools him into thinking I'm OK.

"Look. Mr. Miles is setting up the fishing gear. Let's go see. Hey, maybe we'll catch something really big." Truman leaves me leaning against the main mast, catching my breath. He's gone to the stern of the boat to join the others, crowded around Mr. Miles and his tackle box. I watch his bare feet, so tender and white, pad across the smooth wooden deck. Not wanting to be left alone, I follow.

Mr. Miles casts the lines and sets the rods, which look like weapons, into holders on both sides of the stern. Nothing happens for a long time, and I get bored with waiting. But as soon as I turn my back, one of the lines jerks and bows. "We got a bite!" somebody shouts. Mr. Miles jumps to it, takes the rod out of the holder, and plays the fish. The reel spins and spins. We can't see anything, the sunlight on the water hurts my eyes. I want to go below but this is a big moment, but I can't tear myself away.

Then Mr. Miles hands the harness and belt to Bastien. Bastien is to have the honors, he gets to be the big man and reel the fish in. He strips his tee shirt off, muscles rippling, and tosses it on the deck. Turning to Colton and Myer, he says something. I can't hear what, but I can imagine. He puts the belt and harness on, like he's girding for battle, like he's a fucking giant slayer. Mr. Miles straps the rod in, and now the rod is, like, part of his body, a giant prick. Mr. Miles is coaching him, they're a team. I hate them.

"Use your body weight, son. Save your arm strength."

"I got this!" Bastien pants. "I got it!" Everybody is cheering him on like this is some kind of Super Bowl instead of a life or death struggle. I'm rooting for the fish to win, hoping it will break free. But Bastien the prick starts reeling him in, little by little, inch by inch.

"Be patient, be strong," Mr. Miles says. "I'm here to help."

Pretty soon the fish breaks the water in one last effort to escape. It's huge. It looks nearly as big as I am, and it's beautiful in its struggle, turning and twisting, trying to free itself. I see a stripe of sunlight on its scales, its dorsal fin looks like a flashing yellow blade. A—what's the word? Those curved blades that pirates have? I wish I could cut the line, but here it comes. Bastien is reeling it in. His bare, broad hero's shoulders are gleaming with sweat.

"Ahi!" Miles yells, wielding the mallet. "Looks like a young one, maybe a hundred pounds. He's a fighter. Stand back everybody, stand back!"

Captain Dan leaves the tiller to help Bastien drag the magnificent monster over the rail and onto the deck where Miles pounds its skull with a mallet. I watch in horror as the blood runs red on the deck. Within seconds the fish turns from a shiny living creature to a corpse. The scales lose their shine, the yellow stripe fades to gray, and now it's just any dead fish like you see in the grocery store.

The skipper lay with his nob in gore
Where the scullion's axe his cheek had shore
And the scullion he was stabbed times four
Yo ho ho and a bottle of rum

The sight of fresh blood has summoned the singing dead men again. I try to block out their rants. If I don't give them power, they'll fade out. They'll go back down into the black hole.

"Hey, James! Come look at this!" It's Ming. She's calling me, she's bubbling over. They all are. Bastien stands like a hero, his bare chest heaving, little tufts of hair growing from his man nipples. Steff hands him a bottle of water, and he throws his head back and drinks it down. God, I hate him.

"Now who will help me clean and gut this baby?" asks Mr. Miles. "How about you, Marty? You're not squeamish, are you? Come on over here and get primal, woman," he teases. Our counselor takes the knife he offers her. She is ready to gut the dead fish, she will do whatever he tells her. I can't watch any more of this destruction.

⚓

We set up the cockpit table, we're going to eat our dinner on deck instead of below in the saloon. I have sworn not to eat any of the murdered fish. But when it's served up raw, sprinkled with sea salt and cracked pepper, I find myself gorging on the still-warm red meat, elbow to elbow with everyone else. Guilty now, I'm as guilty as they are. But strangely enough, I'm famished.

Chapter 7

Someone is banging on something—on the side of the ship?

Look, and it cannot be seen. Listen, and it cannot be heard.

The voice is from the black hole. It's not English. It's another language, but somehow I understand it. But I don't want to. Shut up and let me sleep.

Laughter. A high-pitched laugh. A girlish giggle, but hoarse. *That's from the* Tao Te Ching, *James. Do you know the* Tao Te Ching?

Go away.

It remains. I can feel it.

Who are you? (I shouldn't ask a question because that will mean I believe in it. Once I do that, it can't be undone.)

I am Yu. Y-U. Can you appreciate the irony?

Do you know my father?

The dead don't interest me. I am only concerned with the living. You, James McCafferty Junior, you interest me. I am Yu. But I want to be you.

Go away. Go back to hell.

Which one? There are so many. Again, the girlish laughter.

What do you want? (Another question—big mistake.)

Sounds never disappear. Once spoken, words never find rest. I want what you have, James.

Now I'm awake, my heart is the banging drum. I'm sweating, I'm struggling to breathe. Open the curtain. What time is it? Must be near dawn. The darkness isn't quite so heavy. From up on deck, the chatter of voices. Not dead voices bouncing around the universe but words fresh out of the mouths of the living. They sound like birds, the chirping of sparrows. I put on my sweat pants and a hoodie and go up on deck to join them. The sky is a bowl rimmed in pink. We watch the sun appear, a blood orange dripping.

❈

Like a school of sharks, we devour our breakfast of fried Spam, scrambled eggs, and fruit cocktail out of a can. Now that I've got my sea legs—and Ming's magic patch behind my ear—everything tastes good. I can't get enough to eat. I know it all has to do with the workings of the inner ear—the hammer, anvil, and stirrup. The cochlear fluid. We learned that in science. Maybe that's where the drummer lives, in my inner ear. He uses the hammer to beat on the anvil. Everything can be explained logically.

We leave the dishes, the chipped enamel plates, the forks with bent tines and scabs of rust to soak while we report to the cockpit for our morning muster. That's what they call it. Muster. Such a curious, old-fashioned expression, like musty, or "must needs." Muster—I can't get it out of my mind. Sometimes words take hold of my tongue and I keep saying them over and over until they sound really weird and don't make any sense. Anyway, our muster station is the cockpit. On bigger ships that carry more passengers and crew, you are assigned a muster station to report to in case of emergency. Say, the ship has struck an iceberg and is sinking. You report to your muster station with your life jacket and prepare to abandon ship. But since there are only ten of us aboard *Good Fortune*, there's only one muster station—and that's in the cockpit. Every morning after breakfast we gather in the cockpit. We count off to make sure everyone's present, just as we would in a real emergency. We put on our life jackets—which aren't really jackets at all, more like horse collars—then we stow them away again in the emergency locker. After that the captain, Mr. Miles, or Miss Marty makes any announcements they might have, and so the day begins.

The sun is already fierce and ricocheting off the big humps of water coming at us from the east. Darts of light pierce my eyes. I can't find my sunglasses, I think Bastien threw them overboard. Boom boom boom, the drummer hits the anvil with his hammer, a steady beat. Like the pink Energizer battery bunny, he goes on and on thumping his drum.

Mr. Miles announces that Captain Dan has given us an assignment. We are each to write and present a report, using the books in the ship's library as our resources. Groans all around. No one is pleased. *School is out. We have our rights.* Bastien is wearing his fuck-you-all face. Colton and Myer cross their arms like they are his goons.

"Why?" Ming asks. "What is the purpose?" I love her for that. For questioning authority. She is so cool, so self-possessed. Superior in every way.

The first mate takes a noisy slurp of his coffee and gives her a quick, humorless smile. "Captain's orders. Captain's whim." He looks from face to face to savor our reaction. "Anyone who chooses not to participate will be keelhauled." His forehead shines with victory, his voice is triumphant. I think he's kidding, but I can't be sure.

"Do you know what it is to be keelhauled?"

We stare dumbly and wait for the inevitable explanation. "Keelhauling was a form of punishment used in medieval Europe. The miscreant was tied up and tossed over the bow of the ship while it was underway. The ship literally ran over him. When they hauled him up from the stern of the ship, all cut and bleeding from scraping across the barnacles, he was a lucky man if he was still alive. Keelhauling was a form of torture, not unlike waterboarding. You all know what waterboarding is, don't you?"

Bastien flexes his pecs and pulls his cocky grin.

"Like, uh, what are we supposed to report on?" Steff talking. Her eyes are rimmed in black, her lashes are a spider's legs. The dark makeup is startling against her milky white skin. Except for her left arm, tattooed in lurid color. Her skin that will soon burn to a crisp. When does she put her smoky eye makeup on, I wonder? In her bunk, behind her curtain? Or is it permanent, some sort of tattoo?

Mr. Miles savors another mouthful of coffee. I watch his Adam's apple rise and fall as he swallows.

"You can report on anything you want. As long as it can be documented by the sources found aboard. Peruse the ship's library during your leisure time, and see what grabs your attention. See what calls out to you.

"Can we work on our reports together?" Colton asks. "In teams?"

"Each one is responsible for writing his or her own report. You can help each other with research if you want. You can discuss your topics among yourself. But each one will give a presentation individually."

Mr. Miles takes off his aviators and cleans them on his faded blue tee shirt, a shirt worn so thin the lettering has cracked and peeled and mostly washed away. The skin around his eyes is white compared to his wood-colored face. I try to see his eyes—you can tell so much from a person's eyes, but he is looking down and all I can make out is the fringe of lashes, long, thick lashes that don't go with his thinning, gray hair. I really want to see his eyes but he hides behind his dark shades again, before I have the chance.

"When? When's it due?"

"Whenever the captain decides it's due. It's like a pop quiz. He could pick one of you to give your report any day. So better get to work on it as soon as you have free time." Mr. Miles glances at his wristwatch. "Which starts now. You have half an hour before our navigation lesson on the foredeck, so get cracking."

He looks at me, as if reading my mind. "Your fears, McCafferty. Examine your own fears. You'll find a wealth of good topics to research in that bag of bones." He taps his temple with his finger. Two fans of polarized light reflect from his dark, impenetrable glasses.

My head throbs. Inside my skull Yu whispers, *Pick me pick me pick me.*

Chapter 8

I've pulled a book off the shelf. *Chinese Mythology: The Gods, Goddesses, Deities and Demons.* It's a big, thick book. The pages are speckled with age spots and feel moist between my fingers. Like I'm reading braille, I can feel the fingerprints of those who have read it before me, and I can smell the oils, the human sweat, clinging to the pages. It reminds me of my grandmother's encyclopedia of the saints, the book that she kept on her coffee table. When I was little and I stayed with her, she'd read me entries from that book. A real treasury of horrors, all those people who were martyred, skinned alive, decapitated, shot through with arrows or burned to death. Their auras, like lemon Life Savers floating around their heads. I hope they're happy in heaven, up there with God and the angels, but they have never said shit to me. Maybe I'm too bad to be saved. Only the pure of heart have a chance.

These Chinese gods, they actually have power. They seem to work independently of the real God. They don't have a pope, that old wizard with the magic ring, but they do have wizards of their own. Apparently they can cause all sorts of mayhem—or they can bring you fantastic luck—and it doesn't seem to require faith or good deeds. It's all according to their whim. But you have to pay them off somehow. You have to offer them food and wine and give them money or make a shrine to them. The Chinese gods don't perform miracles for free.

I'm trying to figure it out. The complex words, the tedious sentences. The book has been translated into English, but sometimes English is a foreign language to me. Reading has always been a struggle. Certain words leap off the page, like they're in bold print, like they're shouting at me. Other words blend in or hide themselves between neighboring words. Some actually become invisible and then pop out again somewhere else, just to fuck with me. And then there are the shape-shifters, those powerful words that conjure up the voices. I can't read those words, I have to cover them with my hand. Reading is so exhausting.

"Oh, you've discovered the Chinese pantheon, I see." Mr. Miles appears beside me, a coil of rope slung over his shoulder. "You'd do well to make as many friends with those guys as you can."

"Friends? Most of them seem pretty cruel."

"With friends like those, who needs enemies, eh?"

My turn to smile. "Yeah."

His mouth turns up on one side. "It's not a very touchy-feely religion. But be open to their small kindnesses. One of them might take pity on you and offer some sort of protection. Don't refuse it. Especially Mazu, goddess of sailors. She's known by various names and worshipped all over the world by the Chinese diaspora."

Die, what? Diaspora. I'm not sure what that word means, but the sound of it is chilling.

"Make sure you get on Mazu's good side," Miles says. "But watch out for the *shui gui*. Those buggers are tricky. And they're everywhere out here. The ghosts of the drowned, just waiting for the unsuspecting sailor to cross over the exact spot where they went down. Superstition has it they can trade places with you, if that happens. They can steal your body and soul."

My skin prickles.

Mr. Miles goes on, "Chinese people take them very seriously. Not like in our culture. Sure, we have Halloween, which is mostly an excuse for little kids to dress up like superheroes and go begging for candy. But traditional Chinese believe in the supernatural. They appease dead people with festivals all through the year. In fact, the seventh month—the seventh lunar month—is the Hungry Ghost Month. *Zhong Yuan Jie.*"

"There's a ghost month?" I hear myself say. Oh, this can't be good.

Mr. Miles nods. "The whole month is inauspicious. For instance, it's considered dangerous to go out alone at night. Especially on the night of the full moon. That's when the ghosts are most active and have the most power."

"When? What month?"

"The seventh lunar month. The fifteenth night of the seventh lunar month is *Yu Lan*, Hungry Ghost Night. On that night the gates of hell open up, and the spirits who live there are free to roam among the living, who offer food and burn fake money—they call it "hell money"—for the ghosts to use in the other world. To buy them off, sort of. Actually, it's a form of ancestor worship. A lot of cultures have similar beliefs and values. The Chinese make floating lanterns and launch them on lakes to guide the ghosts of their ancestors back to the other world."

"But ghosts don't like flames. What happens to them?"

"To what?"

"The floating lanterns."

He shrugs. "I don't know. I guess, well, eventually they catch fire and sink. It's the act of lighting and launching them, the visual image it makes—that's what's important. It's the symbolism. The ancient ritual that gives it meaning. And it's quite a sight to behold. Maybe we'll celebrate Hungry Ghost Month on *Good Fortune*. We can make lanterns and launch them on little rafts we make and have a contest to see whose lasts the longest. It'll be fun. What do you say?"

"When does this happen?"

Mr. Miles stops to think. He scratches his ear. "It's a summer festival. If I'm not mistaken, it would be mid-August this year. I'll have to check. The Chinese have a rather complicated calendar, a lunisolar system."

"A festival? I don't know if we should stir things up any more. What if—"

The first mate puts his hand on my shoulder in big brother fashion. "Don't take it too literally, kiddo. And don't get lost inside that book right now. You'll have plenty of time to learn about China's gods and ghosts." He makes a fist and bumps my shoulder. "Look, I'm getting ready to teach a knot class up on deck in a couple of minutes. Much more practical. You'll need to know how to tie a half hitch and a bowline, for sure." He's gone and I hear his footsteps above on the deck.

Mazu? *Shui gui?* Hungry ghosts? I want to go up on deck with the others, but I've got to find out how to protect us, what can be done. If anything.

There is a bureaucracy in this universe so immense, James, and so intricate, you'll be lost without my help. Never mind Mr. Miles. What does he know? I'll teach you which gods and ghosts to rely on.

"I don't need them. I'm not Chinese."

The sound of him laughing, that girlish giggle. *Oh, you're much more Chinese than you realize. You'll soon forget this short, unremarkable life. It will seem like a dream. Now, turn the page. This is Jade Yu-ti, the Supreme Emperor, the heavenly counterpart of the earthly emperor. The Supreme Emperor is our creator, but he doesn't concern himself with us. He is above all of that. The human emperor makes sacrifices to him twice a year, to keep his favor. Turn the page, please. Now, the kitchen god and his consort, they're very involved in the day-to-day goings on and they are very popular among the peasantry but—please turn the page—it is the fairies whom I find the most useful, although some are malicious. Here, you see a beautiful fairy who lives in the trees. You can generally tell a fairy by the feet. They never wear shoes.*

Fairies? I'm thinking Tinkerbell. I'm thinking Tooth Fairy. Fairies are gay. I flip forward a few pages to a full-page spread picturing two robed men wearing tall hats. Their faces are made up—one in white, the other in black. Their eyes bulge and they stick their long tongues out, like eighties rock stars, like Kiss.

These are the guards of hell. The Black Guard of Impermanence and the White Guard of Impermanence. You'll want to avoid them. Please turn the page.

"Who is this headless guy? Wú Tóu Guí. Is he, like, Saint James?" Agrippa chopped off James's head and his body was sailed in a rudderless, empty boat to Spain.

I don't know about your saints, and I don't know about Spain, though I'm eager to learn. Wú Tóu Guí is just a type of ghost, one who was executed by beheading. They're very troubled about their heads, but not usually harmful. Not very useful either. Turn the page. There are more ghosts, so many more you need to know.

My eyes fall on a category for which there is no illustration.

Shui gui—Water ghosts. The vengeful spirits of those who drowned and live under the water. They lure unsuspecting—

Suddenly a gust of wind comes in through the porthole, and the page I'm reading flutters out of my fingers. I lose my place. Freaked out, I close the book. On the cover is a kind, smiling woman carved out of jade. Her eyes look down. She looks kindly but sad, like Mary, mother of Jesus.

That's Quan Yin, the goddess of compassion. I don't think she ever knew I existed. The voice sighs regretfully. *This book is a bad translation. You can't believe everything it says. To know the gods and ghosts, you have to live with them. You'll see.*

"James!" I hear my name, but it's not my father calling me. It's Mr. Miles. "McCafferty! Get your ass up here with the rest of the crew. It's time to learn some knots."

⊞

It's good to be up on deck in the fresh air and sunshine, playing with a piece of rope. Myer is really good with the knots, he's a whiz at it. Mr. Miles and Miss Marty praise him, and he's pleased, though he tries to act like, whatever. I'm not too good at the knots, but Ming slides over next to me, and we do it together—make a loop, the rabbit comes up the hole, around the tree and back down the hole. Now pull tight. Her hands are smaller than mine and quicker, but following the little story about the rabbit, I think I've got it.

"A bowline is a handy little knot," Mr. Miles says. "It never slips, it never jams, and it's easy to undo. A bowline could save your life someday." He looks at mine. "Good work, McCafferty. You just needed the right teacher. Now then, if you all think you've got the hang of the half hitch and the bowline, try it with your eyes closed. Try it one handed. You need to be able to tie these knots in your sleep, people. Once you can do six or seven of the easy ones, I'll teach you a few Chinese knots. They're mostly used for decorative purposes."

I want to sit here all day next to Ming and play with the rope, making the rabbit come up the hole, around the tree, and back down. It relaxes me, now that my hands know what to do. I forget all about Chinese gods and ghosts until after supper when everybody is starting to work on their reports. I want to read more about the water ghosts, the *shui gui*. And Hungry Ghost Month. I need to learn more about the goddess of sailors, what was her name? Mazu? And the goddess of compassion, the smiling face on the cover. But where's the book? It's not on the table where I left it. It's not on the shelves. Who took it? And why?

Chapter 9

Mr. Miles says this is our tenth day at sea. He's lying. We've been at sea for months. Maybe years.

The whole world is blue, above and below. The ocean is a mirror for the sky, or maybe the sky is the mirror for the ocean, but don't believe any of it. It's all done with mirrors, you can't trust your own eyes out here. I found the book I was looking for under my own pillow, but I didn't want to read it anymore. I needed to get rid of it, so I burned it, I set it on fire. It was up on deck during my night watch when no one was looking. I lit the pages, and when I couldn't hold onto it anymore, I dropped it overboard.

The next morning the book turns up again, under my pillow, all damp and covered with salt crystals. Someone—some*thing*—wants me to keep this book. So it stays under my pillow, but I don't want to read it.

Sometimes it feels like we're not going anywhere. The boat rocks, I feel the wind, I see the water rise up and sink down, rise up and sink down. Clouds come and go, but nothing really changes. We're stuck in some kind of time warp. It's yesterday again and again.

If I don't think of what's underneath us, I'm OK. The ocean is, like, miles deep here. The deepest part of the ocean is the Marianas Trench—somewhere northwest of our present position. At night when I'm in my bunk listening to the rush of water against the hull, it feels like we're going downhill really fast.

Down, down, at an incredible speed, like we're riding the roller coaster to hell. In the morning I'm surprised to find us still on the surface.

I sleep with all my clothes on. That way I'm ready to go on deck for my watch. I'm ready at a second's notice to abandon ship when it becomes necessary, I'm ready to put on the orange life vest and jump into the lifeboat. Ready to reach out for the Coast Guard rescuer dangling from the rope and reaching for my hand. Being ready at all times helps keep me calm. It sands the raw edges of my fear and helps me fall asleep. Sometimes I sleep deeply, like I'm dead, blissfully unaware of anything. And sometimes I dream.

This night I'm visited by a barefoot child with an axe. I hear it coming, dragging the blade along the wooden deck. Boy or girl, I don't know. It has long white hair, like the ghost of Christmas past. Now it's suspended over me, hovering like a guardian angel. Only instead of a harp, it's holding a weapon.

For you, it says, but in the other language. It looks at me wearily, like I have caused it a lot of work. I think it's the one who brought the book back. And now, with a little hand as cold as stone, it touches my arm. It offers me a pendant, a mirror on a silken cord. A mirror is set in stone. The pendant spins slowly, the mirror reflects little glimmers of light. The angel wants me to have it. Why? It's a talisman. It puts the pendant around my neck and arranges the mirror so that it's lying on the center of my chest. It's heavier than it looks. I touch it. The pendant is cool and smooth on the mirror side, rough on the back, like a carving. I can't see what the carving is—there's not enough light—but I can feel the grooves and the ridges with my fingers.

Keep it on your person, always. The mirror reflects evil and sends it back to the evildoer. Keep Mazu next to your heart where she will hear your prayers. Remember James, there are those who want what you have.

Now I'm rising up through the deep water, coming up for air, still clutching the talisman around my neck. Break the surface and breathe. Breathe! Awake. I'm awake, still clutching, but my hand is empty. The pendant is gone.

⊰╪⊱

Cooking and cleaning take up a fair amount of time. I don't mind the chores, they keep my mind focused and at ease. I do miss my iPod and the music I pump into my head to drown out the voices. Without it I have to hum, and some people find that annoying.

I like it best when I'm near Ming, when we're working side by side. And Truman, I feel easy with him. I think he likes Ming too, in his own way. And she's nice to both of us. It's not like she thinks either of us is hot, but I wish she would. Me, anyway.

Today the three of us have galley duty. Best day ever. We're washing up the breakfast dishes and setting up for lunch. The others are all on deck, we have the saloon to ourselves. The sink looks like a giant wok. It's a big bowl made out of hammered steel, and you fill it with a foot pump that brings in the ocean water. Fresh water is way too valuable to waste on dishes. To rinse, Truman dips them into a bucket of salt water and puts them in the bamboo drying rack. His is the easiest job. Ming wipes them dry and stows them away in the cupboard. We're standing side by side, a little assembly line of dishwashers. I wish I was rinsing so I could stand next to Ming, who is drying. That is the only thing that makes this task anything less than perfect. We're talking, asking questions, curious about each another. What music we like, what movies we've seen. How we ended up here.

Ming says she's an only child. Adopted. Her parents are doctors. Her mom's a pediatric heart surgeon, her dad's a neurosurgeon. Very busy, very important. They are not Chinese.

"My parents want me to learn my native culture and stuff, but they couldn't care less about it themselves. Sometimes I think I'm their little project, some sort of perpetual exchange student."

"I wish I was adopted," Truman says.

"No you don't." She shakes her head, her hair swings. "I was a disappointment to my parents from the day they got me."

"Why?" I ask.

She shrugs.

"Because you're a girl?" Truman says.

"Duh! You can't get anything but girls from China. At the time, they were giving us away like candy. No, they knew they were getting a girl, but it was a baby girl they wanted. An infant, not a five-year-old with a cleft palate. But what could they do, refuse me? No. When you become a parent you take what you get." She grabs another tin plate from the rack and wipes it furiously. "Besides, they're surgeons, and in America a cleft palate is easily repaired. They know people, they have friends—they had my deformity fixed, first thing. Before they even took me home, we checked into the hospital."

A thin white line runs from the bow of her lip to her nose. I'd like to touch it.

"I talked funny. I had a major speech impediment," she says. "Even after the surgery it took a year of therapy until I could talk normally."

"Did you speak Chinese?"

"My parents said I did. I really don't remember. I was only five. But sometimes I dream in Chinese. I think it's Mandarin, actually."

"What do you dream about?" I want to know.

"Say something in Chinese," says Truman, swishing a cup around in the rinse bucket.

She laughs. "I can't. I mean, I can understand it while I'm dreaming, but when I wake up, it all goes out the window. It evaporates, right along with the dream."

"Then how do you know you dream in Chinese?"

She shrugs and tosses her shiny hair. "I just know. Somehow."

I feel bumps of joy rise on the skin of my arms. "In your dreams does it seem like you're remembering another life? A past life—or a parallel existence?"

"Yeah, kind of. But it's not as complete as this one. I mean, it feels very real, but it's limited. And it doesn't make sense. Well, at the time it does, but when I wake up I'm left with—"

She searches the air for the right words. "Crumbs. I'm left with crumbs. And as soon as I sit up, the crumbs scatter into the sheets, and then all that's left is a memory. But it feels as real as any other memory."

"It's called vivid dreaming," I say. "When you know you're dreaming, but it feels very real. It's interactive dreaming. You can change the direction of the dream, you can take control. Lucid dreaming is the first step to astral projection. It's the first step to discovering who you really are. Or who you were in the past."

She doesn't say anything to that, and neither does Truman. I've probably said too much, and now she thinks I'm weird. I don't want her to think that, so I change the subject.

"Where did you live in China? Before you were adopted?" I hand another plate to Truman to rinse. It's a pointless question because I know nothing about China. I just want to hear her talk.

Ming shrugs. "An orphanage. Some little village I can't pronounce. My parents have a whole file. We're supposed to go visit next summer."

"Do you remember anything about it?"

"I remember the first time I saw my parents, their faces all pale and pinched. I thought they looked horrible, but maybe they were just jet-lagged." She laughs. "It's a long flight from Manhattan. I remember they seemed so tall, towering over me. Their noses looked like buzzard beaks. I remember being scared. But they bought me off with a toy panda bear. My little Bobo, I still have him at home on my bed."

"I still don't understand why you were a disappointment to your parents," I say.

Ming picks up another dripping plate from the rack. "Any number of reasons, take your pick. They wanted an adorable infant with a high IQ and a built-in Asian work ethic. But instead they got a five-year-old with a cleft palate. And an attitude. The speech thing was fixed with surgery and therapy. But my attitude got worse. And basically, well, the bottom line is I'm here because I flunked algebra this past semester."

"You're kidding me! You're here because you flunked algebra?"

"Well." She shrugs. "That, and being a klepto. At least, that's what they think I am. A compulsive thief." Her mouth twists into a smile.

"What'd you lift?" Truman asks.

Another shrug. "A couple of things, here and there. Nothing valuable."

"What's the best thing you've ever stolen?" Truman hands her another dish to dry.

She grins. "A bunny rabbit."

"A bunny rabbit? You stole a bunny rabbit?"

I am so relieved. I don't want Ming to be a thief. Stealing a bunny rabbit is not a terrible crime. "There are rabbits in New York City?"

Her face lights up. "I lifted it out of an Easter window display at FAO Schwartz. Just reached over the barrier and picked one up. Nobody saw me. I put it in my backpack and took it home."

Truman is clearly disappointed. "That doesn't count. They were probably giving them away, weren't they? Nobody wants rabbits. They're pests. People shoot rabbits. They hunt them with twenty-gauge shotguns although 410s are popular too. And French people eat rabbits. *Lapin.* It's a delicacy over there. Like snails. Which they call escargots."

"Whatever, Truman. But taking a bunny rabbit is not a crime. Not a serious one."

"That's the point." Ming inspects the dish in her hand, finds a smear, and rubs it off with the dish towel. "I steal worthless things. Stuff nobody else wants. To me, it's valuable. But my parents are mortified, they are so freaked out about it. I think they'd deport me—if they could. Send me back where I came from."

"They can't do that, can they?"

Another shrug of her slim little shoulders. "We'll see. They wanted an Olympic gymnast or a prodigy teen chess champion for a daughter. Somebody special. They made me take music lessons, hoping I would become a concert pianist, or a first chair violinist—the concertmaster—but I chose the clarinet. The lowly clarinet." She sighs. "It's not even a solo instrument. Mozart composed some concertos for the clarinet, and then there was Artie Shaw and Bennie Goodman who did crazy things with it. But all of that is ancient history. Nobody appreciates a clarinet these days—least of all, my parents. But they said I could choose my instrument, and that's what I chose. I think at this point my mother and father would settle for an average kid. OK, maybe slightly better than average—say, top third of the class. But I can't even pull that off. I refuse to excel at algebra, and I'm only mediocre at clarinet. A mathematician or a musician I definitely am not."

"Who are you, then? What *are* you good at?"

She looks at me sideways, with a shy smile like the Mona Lisa. "I'm a rabbit thief. I'm good at disruption and subversion. I'm an anarchist."

Truman busts out a laugh. "To be an anarchist, you'll need an arsenal. I can show you some good weapons. Well, I could if I had my computer and Wi-Fi. But I can draw you some sketches, give you some stats. Weapons are my specialty."

Doodle doodle dee, that's Ming laughing. She sounds like a clarinet. "No, thanks! I was just kidding, Truman. But maybe that's what my parents are afraid of." She stares at the chipped china plate she's holding, like it's a mirror. She cocks her head to one side. "Susie, my nanny, went back to China to see her family, and my parents don't trust me to spend the summer unattended. That's really why I'm here. Well, that—and to punish me for failing algebra. Can you imagine not trusting a sixteen-year-old to be alone? Actually, I do miss my nanny. She was my friend, possibly my only friend." Ming reaches for the cupboard to put the clean plate in the stack. She has to stand on her toes.

"But hey, enough about me," she says. "Truman's the one we have to worry about. He's the one who has an obsession with guns and explosives. We can only pray he doesn't snap and kill us all one day." She ruffles his hair, gone curly and out of control. She pinches his ear. "Promise you won't ever do that, Truman. Ever."

His face is bright pink and he smiles, staring at the dripping fork in his hand. "I promise."

"If you ever get the urge to shoot somebody, call me up and I'll talk you out of it." She puts her arm around him and gives him a squeeze, and although he shrinks and turns his face, he likes it, I can tell. I wish it was me she was hugging, but I know she's just being sisterly to Truman—it was that kind of hug. Now she turns to face me and points her finger at me, touching my chest.

"What are you here for, James? You've never said."

"Me? I'm here for the team-building experience, the adventure of a lifetime," I quip, quoting the blurb from the website. "And because my mother wants me gone."

"What about your father? Is he in the picture?"

"Well, he's in the picture, yes. But he's dead."

Her face crumples. "Oh, I'm so sorry. I didn't even think that—"

"That's OK." I don't want Ming feeling sorry for me, no way. "I mean, it's been a while. He's been dead awhile, so I'm used to it." Her face is red, she's embarrassed. I don't want her to think I'm some poor fatherless freak. "I mean, we all have to die sometime, right?" I say. "He just died a little sooner than most fathers."

There's an awkward silence while she looks down at her shoes, her sporty water sandals. She's thinking of something to say.

"So what are your plans, James? What do you want to do with your life once you get out of school?"

I have no plans. Nothing comes to mind. I mean, sometimes I've thought I wanted to be this or that, but nothing comes to me right now. My mind is like the ocean, deep and filled with amazing creatures, but at any given time if you stare at it, you see nothing at all. Nothing but random reflections of light. That's my brain right now.

I make a jester's face. Try to impress her with a smart-ass attitude. Like Bastien's. "Stayin' alive, that's my plan. One day at a time."

One last pot to be scrubbed. I will wash it slowly, I don't want this to end.

"Oh, come on! Tell me something real. Like, who do you admire? If you could be somebody else—anybody—who would you be?"

I want to impress her with my choice, but I'm drawing a blank. I can't think of anybody I want to be except a better version of myself. I blank out, hoping one of the voices in the black hole will leap out and speak for me. Instead, I hear Yu snickering. *Tell her*, he whispers. *Tell her about me.*

Truman says he would be an elite member of the Special Forces, the one who took out Osama Bin Laden. But Ming is looking at me. She wants to know who I would be, and I almost say Bastien, but I would never admit that.

"Admiral Zheng He," I blurt out. "The guy Miles was talking about. The one who led the Ming emperor's treasure fleet. Ha! Ming, like you, Ming! I'd be your admiral, at your command."

Ming's eyes dance and she's trying not to laugh. "He was a eunuch, you know. Zheng He was castrated."

The heat creeps up my neck, my face must be glowing red. God, could I be any more stupid? Why did I not know that?

Truman is laughing, he thinks it's hilarious.

"Shut up, Truman," I say, but he's still snickering. Mr. Miles didn't say he was a eunuch, did he? Maybe I wasn't listening. I'm not exactly sure what a eunuch is, but I'm pretty sure it means he's had his nuts cut off. I think that's what castrated means. Like a dog that's been neutered. No balls. And I just said I'd like to be a man with no balls.

"Lots of the generals and admirals of the old Chinese dynasties were eunuchs," says Ming, who obviously was paying attention when Miles was droning on. "But they were the fiercest of warriors."

"I thought you said you weren't smart," I grumble. Fragments of a dream return, a boy's voice remembered. The drumming starts up in my head.

"I never said I wasn't smart. I'm just not smart in the way my parents want me to be."

Suddenly Ming snaps the dishtowel on my arm in a playful way and I grab it. We play a little tug of war. She's smiling wickedly, the bridge of her nose wrinkles, and her eyes are lit up like glowing coals. "Being a eunuch had its advantages, you know."

"I don't even want to know." But I do want to know, I want to know everything. I want her to hit me again with the dish towel.

"The eunuchs got to sleep with the concubines. Since they couldn't knock them up, the emperors didn't care."

"I don't want to talk about eunuchs. I was only kidding."

She wraps the dish towel around my neck, pretending like she's going to choke me. "Come on, James! What's your dirty little secret? We all have one."

I blush pink like Truman did when she teased him and ruffled his hair. But I can't tell her why I'm here. I won't.

⚜

The dishes, silverware, pots, and pans have all been dried and stowed in the cupboard. The dirty water has been drained out into the ocean, the sink wiped clean, and the sea cock under the sink turned off so water doesn't come in and flood the cabin. The lower deck has been swept and the sour smelling dish towel hung to dry.

Now we're supposed to resupply the food from the storeroom below. According to the list, we need rice, cooking oil, dried mushrooms, and Spam. We eat Spam nearly every day. Mr. Miles says Spam is good boat food because it provides protein and fat, and it keeps for ages without refrigeration. Today's dinner calls for stir-fried rice with cubes of Spam. I guess when you're hungry you'll eat anything. And as Miles likes to point out, there's no McDonald's at sea.

We have a few fresh vegetables. Cabbages, onions, and garlic are strung from the deckhead in nets to let the air circulate. They don't need refrigeration. The outer layers turn black, but you just peel them off until you get to the unspoiled part. Our parents would be horrified, but no one has gotten sick from the food. We have eggs too, and we have to turn them over in their crates every few days so that they last longer, that's what Mr. Miles says. He says the Chinese preserved most things by salting and drying, and we've got a lot of weird food items stored down below. Like dried cuttlefish and salted dried plums.

Nobody likes to go down to the locker to bring up more food. It's pitch black down there and so stuffy. That's because it's practically airtight, it's below the waterline, so no portholes. And nothing is labeled. You just have to root around until you find what you're looking for.

Truman has pulled a book off the shelf—*Medieval Weaponry*. He's stretched out on the settee, studying it. Ming doesn't want to go down to the locker either. She goes to her bunk and comes back with a plastic case, a zippered Hello Kitty pouch. "I'm going to paint my nails," she announces.

"I'll go down," I say, not wanting to at all.

"OK, you go. Thanks, James." She sits down at the table, fanning her hands in front of her to examine them. Her tiny, bitten-off fingernails have traces of dark blue polish. "Hmm. What color should I be?"

"I'll go," I say again. Still hoping one of them will offer to help me. I should make Truman come with me, but I don't want to look like a sniveling ball-less eunuch. "Just make sure nobody comes in and closes the hatch while I'm down there."

"Don't worry, James. I'll make sure the hatch stays open. Oh, and just in case there is something evil down there, I'll let you wear this for protection." She reaches down the front of her tee shirt and pulls out something—a necklace, a pendant—from its hiding place. A cold shiver runs through me. "This will deflect malicious ghosts and evil doers." She stands up and places it around my neck, the same round mirror set in carved jade I received in my dream. White jade, I see now in the daylight.

"The mirror reflects the bad energy away. It's a feng shui thing. And on the reverse side," she flips it over with her tiny fingertips, "the goddess of sailors, I forget her name." We're face to face, so close it's like we're going to kiss.

"Mazu." The word floats out of my head.

"Something like that, yeah."

My heart is hammering away, it's trying to bust down the walls of my chest. "Where did you get this? Did the barefoot child with the axe come to you last night?" Then it occurs to me, Ming took it from me while I was sleeping. Like she took the rabbit. She's a thief, she said so herself. But I'm glad she's been wearing it next to her skin. The stone is still warm from resting in the space between her breasts. I feel like she is a queen, and she has just made me her knight by placing her talisman—my talisman—around my neck.

"You sure have some crazy dreams, James. I brought the pendant with me. It was a gift. Susie gave it to me before she left for China. She said it would bring me good fortune."

Ming turns away from me and sits back down on the bench. She reaches into her zippered pouch and pulls out a handful of tiny bottles of nail polish, lining them up in a row on the dining table. An assortment of colors: silver, magenta, deep purple, midnight blue, black, lime green, aquamarine. "I think I'll do a lighter shade of blue." She picks up the aquamarine and turns the bottle between her fingers. It's filled with glitter, it sparkles in the sunlight coming through the porthole. "This one's called Caribbean Blue. Do you like it?"

"It's beautiful."

"Yeah. It's the color I wish my eyes were."

"I like your eyes the color they are."

"Brown is boring. Most people on the planet have brown eyes."

"But there's so many shades of brown. Your eyes are almost black. Like Coca Cola. And just as refreshing." Look, I've made her smile.

"What color are your eyes? Come here. Let me see."

I sit next to her and hold my breath while she looks into my eyes. I feel like she can see inside me.

"Your eyes are the color of acorns. With little gold flecks. What about you, Truman? What color are your eyes?" She is still looking at my eyes, and I still can't breathe.

"Gray," he says, not looking up from his book.

Ming turns back to her nail polish, releasing me. She shakes the bottle of Caribbean Blue and then twists off the lid. The sharp chemical smell makes my head whirl. I look over her shoulder as she bends her head close, concentrating. Dips the brush, wipes it against the inside of the bottle, and then makes three quick strokes across her tiny thumbnail. "Don't forget to take the flashlight, James," she says, without looking up. "It's dark down there in the rabbit hole."

"You mean hold," says Truman. "It's called a hold, not a hole."

"I know. I was being ironic," says Ming, rolling her eyes and smiling at me like it's a private joke between us. My heart jumps. "You are so literal, True."

Reluctantly I leave my seat next to Ming. I pick up one of the flashlights stowed in the wooden box on the bookshelf. I open the hatch in the floorboards. Standing at the top of the ladder, I breathe deep. It's like diving into a cold swimming pool. I've got to pump myself up for it. I think of Ming, I'll do it for her.

"Watch out for zombies," taunts Truman from behind his book.

The hatchway is narrow. A fat person would never fit, but I'm skinny. I go down backward. Slowly. Step-by-step, my hands gripping the rope railings, my feet feeling for the rungs of the ladder. I wait for my eyes to adjust to the dark and then turn the flash light on and aim it, like it's a gun. Stacks and stacks of crates, a crooked passageway through the center. Most of the crates aren't marked, it's a guessing game as to what's inside. I start to forage.

I'm not alone, I know it. I feel them. I'm afraid I'll see them. I start ripping lids off of crates randomly. *Hurry! Get your butt in gear*, Dad used to say. Dried beans, more beans, nothing but beans. Here's something, what the hell is this? Some kind of dried stuff—is it mushrooms? Shine the light on it—it looks like crooked brown fingers and ears. Forget it, I'm not eating that! Move on, another crate. What's in this? Is it rice? Yes, rice! Grab a burlap bag and stick it under my arm like a football. Now for the Spam.

It smells like decay, something's rotten. They're waking up, I can feel their eyes, their roving eyes. Soon they'll see me. Another crate, what's in this one? Nuts? I don't know, I'm looking for the cooking oil. Where's the stupid cooking oil?

Oh shit, what's that! Something black scuttles across my foot, it's a—a centipede, must be six inches long. It disappears into the darkness. Centipedes hate light and they sting like a mother, that's what Mr. Miles told us. The ones in the tropics are heinously big. They eat cockroaches and when they run out of cockroaches, they eat each other. Shine the light down so I don't step on any. A cloud of cold air. Where's that coming from? I'm cold—*cold*—like my body heat's been sucked out of me. The flashlight flickers and dies. It's pitch black, my heart swells up and sticks in my throat. I'm shaking the flashlight, smacking it against my hand. No good. Something is drawing the power from the batteries, something is taking the heat out of my body. I don't see anything, but I can feel them, hundreds of them, and I can hear the echoes of their last screams. Their pleas and prayers. They drowned, they were slaughtered, they were burned. They didn't go down easy, they struggled all the way. They want air, they're hungry for air, they want to be alive. This is the black hole of Calcutta, this is the black hole in my mind, this is the hold of *Good Fortune* where the dead people, the *shui gui*, wait to be born again.

I stumble toward the ladder, toward the square of light above. Only the pendant is protecting me. I feel it heavy around my neck, guarding my heart, the portal to my soul. But there are so many of them, and there he is, the boy whose voice has found its way inside my head. I feel grasping fingers at the back of my neck. My scalp tingles, fizz from a soda can. Somebody is grabbing at the pendant. Somebody is trying to choke me with it. I feel it tight around my neck. Can't breathe! Reach in my pocket for the lighter. They fear fire, it slows them down. But the lighter slips out of my hand. I think I dropped it, I don't see it. Just get the hell out of here, James! Up the ladder—at least I still have the rice. They're reaching for me, they're pulling at me. Trip and smack my shin on the ladder—hurry! Don't stop! Toward the light!

Chapter 10

"What the hell happened here? Somebody get married and didn't invite me?" Mr. Miles asks.

"A bag of rice broke." I'm holding the dust pan as Ming sweeps up. "Sorry. I accidentally dropped it." I'm still shaking. I can hardly speak.

"What's the matter, McCafferty? It's not like I'm going to flog you for spilling some rice."

"They're down there."

"Who's down there?"

"You know." I want to tell him they took my lighter, but I can't because we're not even supposed to have lighters.

"Centipedes? I warned you. Did you get stung?"

"I'm not talking about bugs."

He grins. "Oh, you mean the *shui gui*?"

"The what?" Ming says. "What are you talking about?" She's still holding the broom. She's holding it carefully so as not to mess up her new Caribbean Blue nails, not quite dry.

"*Shui gui*," Mr. Miles says. "Water ghosts. According to Chinese mythology, people who drown or die at sea are doomed to remain in their dark and watery hell until a living person passes over the spot where they went down. Then, if they're powerful enough, the ghost can change places with the living person." He gives me that smug grin again. "You'll find it all here on the bookshelves. If I'm not mistaken, McCafferty is going to give us a full report when the captain calls on him."

Truman is scornful. "Ghosts are for kids on Halloween. They don't really exist. We should do our reports on real stuff."

I wish I were Truman, smart but blind to the other world. I envy him his blindness, his isolation. He plays with his fact collection, he shuffles random bits of information and deals them out like playing cards. Statistics are his poker chips: red, white and blue.

"OK, Truman, next time *you* can go get supplies. I'm not going down there anymore."

Mr. Miles sits down and launches into another lecture. "Maybe *you* don't believe in them Truman, but most of humanity has believed in ghosts, and many people still do. Especially the Chinese. They've developed all sorts of rituals to appease them. They burn fake money, and they put out food for them. These superstitions, these beliefs, are an important part of Chinese culture, a culture that's thousands of years older than ours. I won't say anymore because McCafferty is going to report on it. I don't want to steal his thunder. What's your topic, Truman? What are you studying?"

Truman's attention has already returned to his book. It's like he doesn't even hear him.

"Truman?"

He looks up from the page.

"I asked you, what are you studying?"

Truman shows him the book's cover.

"Ah, medieval weaponry—a favorite subject of mine. We can make a catapult—we've got everything we need on board. Lob some old cannon balls out into Old Blue. We can make some flaming cabbage bombs. What do you say, Truman? Does that sound like fun?"

Mr. Miles is changing the subject, but he knows what's up. He knows all about them. Maybe this is all a setup. Maybe that's why we're here, so the *shui gui* don't get him. Maybe that's our purpose, to be decoys. Or maybe the Chinese spirits have used Captain Dan and Mr. Miles to deliver us to them.

We, being younger, with more of our lives ahead of us. Maybe Miles and Captain Dan are *shui gui* themselves. My mind is racing in circles, it's like a carnival ride that never stops. I want off but the operator won't shut it down. I'm inside this whirling cage, my skull. And I can't get out. The only way out is to die, and maybe not even then.

"Can I have my pendant back?" Ming looks up from her aqua blue fingernails. "It was a gift."

It's not yours, Ming, I'm thinking. *The fairy put it around my neck, and you took it from me. But I like you. Maybe I love you, I want you to have it. You have no idea about the devils waiting down below.*

"Sure," I say, making my mouth smile.

"I just put another coat of polish on my fingernails. They're not dry yet. Would you?" She bends her head forward. She wants me to put it around her neck, and I feel a little burst of joy. It's like we're in a relationship, and I'm giving her my pendant to wear so she'll be protected from them who want to drag us down. Now I know Ming will be saved, if not me. Mazu will save her.

Chapter 11

We're all on deck learning how to use the sextant, a thing that measures angles, like how high the sun is above the horizon. Truman and Ming are the only ones paying attention. I can't focus on what Mr. Miles is saying, it's all a bunch of blah, blah, blah. I don't care about our coordinates. It's pointless. Knowing our latitude and longitude won't mean anything if the ghosts want to bring us down. All I want is to get off this boat alive. I want to do something awesome with my life, but I don't know what. I'm not really good at anything, not yet. I'm afraid I'm just a microphone for the voices. There's pills for that, I know. Pills that muffle the voices, but then I wouldn't hear my father anymore either. And I might not hear my own voice, my spirit guide. My conscience.

The best days of my life were the ones spent on my grandmother's farm. She lived in Maryland, outside of Hagerstown, near Antietam National Battlefield. Dad and I stayed a few summers with her when he was between jobs, looking for work. Me and Kyle, an older boy who lived on the neighboring farm, we'd spend long July days playing in the Civil War woods, damming the creek with rocks and logs, making ourselves a little pond, building bridges with dead branches.

"How come you call this the Civil War woods? It's private property, you know. It belongs to my grandfather. It's not part of the battlefield," Kyle said one day as we were walking toward home on Butcher's Lane, all sweaty, our shoes soaking wet and covered with river mud.

I was surprised by the question. Did he really not know? Wasn't he aware of the shadows roaming through the trees alongside us? Doesn't he see the black man who always followed us as far as Gran's mailbox? Who was following us, even now?

"I call it the Civil War woods because of all the soldiers roaming the woods. Like the guy whose arm got shot off by a cannon ball, the one with the empty, tattered sleeve. I think his name is Jim." I jerked my thumb over my shoulder.

Kyle looked at me like I was crazy. "What soldier? What are you talking about? Who's Jim?"

Apparently Kyle wasn't aware of them, just as they weren't aware of us, except in a very vague way. I always thought it was just a matter of paying attention. How to explain? It's like describing red to somebody who is color-blind. It was probably the first time I realized I was different.

"This Jim—is he real? Is he, like, a homeless guy? A bum? A Civil War reenactor?"

"No." I kicked a stone and sent it flying. "He's from the spirit world. He's a residual haunting. A ghost. But I don't think he sees us." Kyle kept giving me little sideways glances, trying to figure out if I was just "bullshitting," as he called it. He did a fair amount of bullshitting himself and always accused me of doing the same.

"Don't worry," I said, biting a little scab off my arm. "Jim won't hurt us. He just wants to go home but can't find his way." The look on Kyle's face told me to shut up. I decided then I couldn't tell him, or anybody, everything I saw and heard. "It would make a good movie, wouldn't it?" I said. "We could play like we're actors in a Civil War movie. Or directors. And Jim can be one of the supporting characters. He gets killed."

Kyle's face brightened. He was relieved. He didn't want to hang out with somebody who didn't know the difference between real and pretend. I realized he was no longer a part of both worlds. This one and the world we called make-believe when we were little. Maybe I never came out of that world, never left it behind. Maybe all little kids can see ghosts, and that's why they're afraid to go to sleep at night. Then most kids outgrow it. Maybe they lose the ability to see and hear spirits just like they lose their baby teeth. But some of us don't lose all of our baby teeth. In fact, I still have two of mine.

"Hey, I got an idea," Kyle said, taking my idea and making it his own like he always did. "Tomorrow, let's play Civil War. We can turn these woods into a battleground. Sharpsburg, which is what the South called Antietam. Or Shiloh, that was a real bloody battle. You can be a Yankee and I'll be a Rebel. I'll be Jeb Stuart and we'll fight each other with muskets and bayonets. And we can video it. We can make our own movie and put it on YouTube. Maybe I can use my Uncle Joe's paintball guns."

"Yeah," I said. "Paintball, that'll be fun." I let Kyle think the whole Civil War thing was his idea, and I didn't say anything more about the soldier Jim or any of the rest of his company. I didn't say anything when I nearly choked on the smell of black powder smoke and bodies rotting in the sun.

We crossed a fence, sliding between the strands of rusted barbed wire. I must've been careless, I got snagged on one of the sharp barbs. Yanking myself free, I ripped my shirt. A little scrap of cloth remained stuck on the barb, a tiny white banner, a flag of truce. Is it still there, I wonder? Or have the birds picked it free? Is Jim still wandering the fields, trying to find his way home? Did the war ever really end, or is it still going on? Is everything still going on?

⊣⊢

After lunch Mr. Miles gives us a history lesson about the battle of Tarawa, a World War II massacre as he describes it, on some remote island south of here.

"Casualties were heavy on both sides, Japanese and American, and there was no possibility of retreat on that sliver of sand and coral." Mr. Miles looks at us from behind his dark glasses to make sure we're listening. I am. I can hear their shouts and screams, those guys fighting each other. For what?

"What were they fighting for?"

Everybody looks at me like I'm stupid. "It was a war, dude," says Myer. As if that explains everything.

"They were fighting for control of the Pacific," Mr. Miles says. "They were fighting for strategic real estate, for islands to be used as naval and air bases. And to revenge the unprovoked attack by the Japanese on Pearl Harbor, our biggest naval base in the Pacific."

"If somebody's arm is blown off by a cannonball, would they die right away, or would it take them a while?" My voice.

Mr. Miles looks at Miss Marty, who makes a face and shrugs. He looks up into the sky as if to find an answer. "Likely it would take them a while to die. Maybe they would live, if they had the right first aid. A tourniquet to stop the bleeding. A good surgeon to close the wound. And antibiotics to prevent infection. But we're not talking particulars here, we're talking about the big picture. The events of history. So let's try to keep on track, OK, McCafferty?"

<hr />

We're sitting on deck in the shade of a canvas awning we've rigged, drinking warm fruit punch from cans, which also isn't as bad as it sounds. It's wet and sweet and tastes good in this heat. The wind has gotten stronger, the first good wind we've had so far, according to Captain Dan, who says we're behind schedule.

Steff and Colton are chosen to raise the mizzen sail. The captain sets the self-steering, a thing he's rigged to keep the tiller on a set course without him having to actually hold it. It only works when the wind is steady and strong. Now the motion of the boat is comfortable, it feels like we're being rocked on one of those old glider things like Gran had on her front porch. We're all on deck, the adults apart from the kids, but all within sight of one another. It almost feels like a holiday—the sun shining brightly on the blue waves, the refreshing breeze, and the puffy white clouds like a herd of sheep on the horizon. I'm whittling a bar of soap into the shape of a cloud.

The girls are playing with each other's hair, French braiding it. Miss Marty is engrossed in a paperback book, and Truman is buried in a ham radio manual.

"So McCafferty, have you seen any dead people recently?" Bastien asks. He's sprawled out alongside his overgrown minions, Colton and Myer. They appear to be sleeping.

"Not today," I say. He's setting me up, he's going to make an ass out of me. None of them really believe. Sometimes they pretend to believe in ghosts, just for a thrill. Like adults, they think it's fun to be scared, to lose control of their senses for a few minutes, for an hour and forty-eight minutes, the length of your average horror movie. But they don't really believe, or if they do, they don't admit it.

The world is so crowded with so many souls, and so many of them seem to be lost or regretful. Maybe we're already ghosts and don't know it. Layers and layers of ghosts, unaware of each other. I think of my lighter, belowdecks in the food storage locker where they reside. I want my lighter back, but I'm afraid to go down there.

⚓

Little by little I'm finding out more about the others. Some of it they share. Much of it I read on their faces, in the color of their energy, the auras they give off. Sometimes I hear between the lines. Intuition, my mother calls it. It's not like I can actually read minds or the future, like Gran could. It's just knowing. I know Colton and Myer are lonely even though they are part of a pack, a wolf pack led by Bastien. I know Steff feels like an outcast. Even though Bastien likes her, she doesn't quite believe she is worthy of him. When Steff looks in the mirror, she doesn't see what I do. She sees something ugly and deformed. Which is sad because she is really pretty, and she has a good heart. I know Ming is lonely too. She wants to be respected. Taken seriously. Loved.

"I know how you feel, Ming," I say, pulling the brim of my hat down to keep out the sun's glare.

"What?" She squints, wrinkling the skin on the bridge of her nose.

"I said I know how you feel."

Her irritation leaps out in a flash of red orange. "No, James, you don't know how I feel. You have no idea how I feel."

"OK, whatever. Sorry." But I do know how she feels. Ming is carrying this dark thing, this stain. It gives a bitter taste in her mouth. She feels like an outsider and she wants to be an insider. Truman too is on the outside. He's orbiting, orbiting, orbiting. The difference is, I don't think Truman minds it. The rest of us are like dogs to him. Nice enough to have around, but lesser beings. Truman doesn't give a shit what the others think of him. But I care.

"Stop it, Truman." I say. "Stop picking your nose."

He pauses, his finger poised midair, maybe remembering that nose-picking is not acceptable. He wipes his hand on his shirt, he's got other things on his mind, things I can't comprehend. Truman tolerates me. Like he tolerates everyone, for the inferior beings we are. He thinks Ming is hot, but that's only biology, his hormones speaking. Honestly, I don't think he'll remember us six months from now. If only we would live that long.

⊰⊱

Night watch. Me and Bastien, together on deck. The two of us alone. The wind is steady out of the east, it fills the fan-shaped sails. It's so reliable we don't even have to hold the tiller, it is lashed into the correct position to keep us on course. The boat creaks and groans like an old woman as she waddles along. Bastien doesn't talk to me, and I don't talk to him. He settles in on the bench for a little nap.

Since Bastien has claimed the helmsman position, I go forward, to the bow, checking the lashings on the lifeboat and water barrels and scanning the dark horizon for the lights of other vessels, even though we've seen nothing since we left Honolulu. The moon has come up and spills its weak white light. Something catches my eye. It looks like a face in the water, but when I look closely, it's gone. It might have been a sea creature—like a jellyfish or a Portuguese man-of-war. Maybe.

I hear something. A rumbling noise growing louder, it sounds like a train. What the hell? Ahead of us, a ship. A battleship. It's huge, it's bearing down on us. We can't avoid it—we're going to hit! I feel a surge go through me, like I've been struck by lightning, and pee is running like a warm river down my leg.

"Ship! Ship dead ahead!" I can barely hear my own words. It's a bad dream. My voice is so weak, and I can't seem to move. "Turn the boat, Bastien! Oh, shit, we're going to hit!" I can't take my eyes off the huge ship, growing larger. I'm a raccoon in the headlights of an oncoming truck. We're doomed.

"What the hell! What's going on?" Captain Dan and Mr. Miles come running all huffing and puffing, their bare feet slapping on the deck. They are too late. They are totally unprepared, they can do nothing to save us.

"McCafferty, what are you talking about?"

"What ship?"

"Where's the ship?"

I point, but it's gone. Vanished before my eyes. All I see now is moonlight like spilled milk on the water. The only sound is the swish of water against the hull and the wind playing over the battened sails. They've disappeared, they've gone back to their own time. They probably weren't even aware of us. They're an echo or an old movie that plays over and over again. I'm so relieved, but embarrassed too.

Everyone on board is wide awake now, everybody is whispering about me. Miss Marty puts the water on for coffee. She talks about the effects of fatigue and sensory deprivation on the mind. She's making excuses for me, but it's making matters worse. Everybody thinks I'm hallucinating again. They think I'm crazy.

"Beware the *shui gui*, mates," Mr. Miles says brightly, going down to the galley to pour himself a cuppa joe, as he calls it. My ears burn. Bastien just looks at me like I'm a piece of fresh, steaming dog shit he stepped in. Which is what I feel like.

"Believe me, kid, we all see things at sea," Captain Dan says, placing his big paw on my shoulder. "Once I saw a man on the foredeck. Which was impossible since I was the only one on the boat at the time. He was naked except for a loin cloth, and he was covered with tattoos from head to foot. Some old

Polynesian navigator he was, chanting in his language, reciting his star chart and calling on his gods. He disappeared when the sun came up. But I know what I saw and what I heard."

I appreciate his story, but kindness from Captain Zombie himself is the last straw. My face feels hot. It's glowing, I am a lighthouse of humiliation. I can't hold them back any more, the tears. There's only one place to go to be alone. Only one place to hide. I crawl into my bunk and pull the curtain, bury my head under my pillow. On deck I hear a burst of laughter.

Chapter 12

Everyone is looking forward to Palmyra, our first landfall. Me, most of all. Palmyra is a speck of land in the middle of the Pacific Ocean—as far away from a continent as you can get. And according to Mr. Miles, it's cursed.

"Do you know why?" he asks. We don't. "Well, go hit the bookshelves and see what you can find out."

I'm thinking Palmyra can't be any more cursed than *Good Fortune* is. It's only a matter of time before they take over. I'm planning on staying behind once I reach land, but I'm not exactly sure how I'm going to pull it off. I'm getting some ideas, though. Herman Melville jumped ship in the Marquesas Islands. He hid out until his ship, a whaler, left without him. I read that in a book called *Typee*, which he wrote in 1846, before he wrote *Moby Dick*. Which I've never read but maybe I will, if I live long enough. Maybe I can do what Herman did, run away and hide. Except I'm pretty sure *Good Fortune* won't leave without me. Maybe I'll accidentally get injured, cut my finger off with a machete or something. Maybe I'll get appendicitis or dengue fever, and they'll have to airlift me out.

We go down to the saloon, we're combing the shelves to find out what we can about Palmyra. We've turned into scholars, hungry for knowledge about our first landfall. What will we do and where will we go, once we get there?

Steff pulls an atlas off the shelf, searches the index, and then opens to the centerfold. "That's the Pacific Ocean and we're right in the middle of it." Palmyra is a dot, even on the blow up of the area, the inset.

"Not very big," says Colton.

"Technically, Palmyra isn't an island," says Truman. "It's an atoll. An atoll is formed as a volcanic island slowly sinks and the coral reef fringe builds around it, forming a lagoon."

Colton pulls another book off the shelf, a binder of handwritten notes. "Says here it was discovered by accident in 1798. This dude, this sea captain named Edmund Fanning, saw it on his way to Asia. Then a couple of years later another ship, the USS *Palmyra*, wrecked there in 1802." He skims down the page. "A Gerrit P. Judd of the ship *Josephine* claimed it for the United States in 1859. He was going to mine guano, whatever that is, but—"

"Bird shit," says Bastien.

"What?"

"Guano is bird shit. And bat shit. It's used for fertilizer."

"And gunpowder," says Truman.

"Apparently they didn't find any shit there at all. So a few years later King Ka—what's-his-name—the Fourth took possession of the atoll and in 1862 it was formally annexed to the Kingdom of Hawaii."

Everybody's talking and reading out loud from different books, all at once. It's exciting, almost like we've discovered buried treasure. Well, not that exciting, but it pulls us together. It gives us a mission.

Truman: "The whole atoll is only about a mile long."

Myer: "Hey, you guys, listen to this! 'In 1816 the Spanish ship *Esperanza* got into a battle with another ship near here. The *Esperanza* was going down, but the Spaniards escaped and somehow brought the gold to shore.'"

Colton: "How come the Spaniards were always sailing around with boatloads of gold?"

Myer: "I don't know. Shut up and listen. They took their treasure to Palmyra and buried it. Then they built rafts and tried to escape."

Steff: "I wonder, why didn't they just take the gold on the rafts with them? Why did they leave it behind?"

Myer: "Maybe there wasn't enough room. Maybe there was so much gold, it was too heavy. I don't know, they probably planned to come back later, with real ships. Maybe they took a little pocketful each and told the king they had to leave the gold behind."

Ming: "So maybe it's still there?"

Bastien: "Could be that's why we're stopping. The Captain and Miles are treasure hunters. I'll bet they have a clue where it is."

Truman: "Or they want to scavenge for World War II artifacts. Rusted guns, unexploded grenades, pieces of fuselage. Stuff like that."

Me: "Finding lost Spanish gold would be way better."

"Oh, but here's the weirdest of all," Steff said, reading the back cover of a beat-up paperback. "Check this out. 'In 1974 a grisly double murder occurred on Palmyra. But only one of the bodies has ever been found.' This is a true story, you guys, this really happened! The author is a lawyer who represented one of the two people on trial for the murder of Mac and Muff Graham. They sailed from California to Palmyra on their yacht, the *Sea Wind*."

Myer: "Maybe we'll find the other body."

Steff: "It says here Palmyra's lagoon is teeming with sharks. The sharks might have eaten it."

"We should divide up into teams and explore," I say, "with shovels and machetes. But we'll have to be careful we don't get dengue fever. It can make you really sick. So sick you'd have to be evacuated."

⊰⊱

Back on deck we watch impatiently as *Good Fortune* creeps along, inch by inch toward our destination. Palmyra is a smudge, a blur on the horizon. If you didn't know it was there, it would be easy to miss. You would sail right on by and not even know it. Except Mr. Miles has the coordinates entered into his pocket GPS. "I see palm trees! And sail boats!" Myer shouts, binoculars to his face.

"Let me see," Colton pleads.

"Wait a minute, I'm not done."

"Yes you are. It's my turn!" Colton reaches for the strap around Myer's neck and Myer pushes him away.

"Stop it!" Miss Marty says. "That's enough! You're acting like two-year-olds." But our counselor is impatient too. She wants her chance to look through the binoculars.

Mr. Miles calls us all together to find out what we've learned about Palmyra. We tell him about the Spanish ship that wrecked and about the double murder of Mac and Muff. "I knew that would get your attention," he says. "Palmyra's real significance is that it was used by the Americans during World War II as a refueling base. Then, for decades after the war ended, it was privately owned. An old hermit caretaker lived there, and it was during those years that the murders took place. Now it belongs to the Nature Conservancy, it's a marine preserve. A haven for birds. Nobody lives there except visiting scientists. A few sailboats stop by on their way to the South Pacific, but shore access is limited."

Then comes the crushing announcement. Mr. Miles says that we're not actually going to Palmyra, we're not even going to anchor in the lagoon. Instead, the plan is to anchor somewhere along the reef, to explore a possible shipwreck site.

"What? No fair!" we protest. There goes my plan to stay ashore.

"Sorry mates, those are Captain Dan's orders. And aboard ship, captain's orders are law." The first mate goes forward to get the anchor ready.

"But why?" Ming tags after him, speaking for all of us. "Why can't we? We're tired of being on the boat." We follow her in a line. We're her platoon, tee shirts wrapped around our heads, sleeves tied behind our heads, a style Bastien started. It's kind of a cross between a rapper's do-rag and a pirate's head gear. We surround Mr. Miles. He's stooped over, shackle in hand, attaching a rusty chain to the bow anchor. We are ready to mutiny.

Mr. Miles looks up from what he's doing. He's annoyed but not threatened by us. "Look guys, it's a wildlife preserve. There's nothing much of interest on shore anyway, and they don't let you go wandering around because it's a protected nesting area for pelagic species. I've been there before, take my word." He turns back to the anchor chain.

"That's wrong," Ming blurts out. "With all due respect, Mr. Miles, we were led to believe we'd be going ashore. We deserve to. We're sick of being cooped up on this boat."

He wipes the sweat off his forehead with the back of his hand and stands up. "Trust me, all the cool stuff is underwater. And that's where we're going." He looks at us through his dark shades, I feel his eyes on us, he is sizing us up. "I'll let you in on a little secret. The Captain and I are going to do some salvage diving tonight. And we don't want to tip our hand. Don't want to have those folks from the Nature Conservancy all over us, running us off the reef. You catch my drift? We're going to have to be a little stealthy here. Now's your chance to be pirates, mates." He says "Arrrrgh" like a pirate, but nobody smiles.

Mr. Miles says we'll be able to go ashore at the next landfall, one of the Line Islands not far south of here. Christmas Island or Fanning. If the wind holds. He promises us a good shore leave if we work hard tonight hauling up salvage from the wreck. "All you kids will have a day of liberty, trust me. You can go ashore, walk into town. You can get drunk on Coca Cola and Fanta, come back with a tattoo—I don't care." There's promise in his smile.

And so we sail right past the main island, the lagoon where Mac and Muff were murdered. We can't see much except palm trees and a few sailboat masts. The captain is steering and Mr. Miles is on the foredeck, keeping an eye out for the reef so we don't run into it. He pulls out his GPS and looks at the chart, folded in his hand. The wind has dropped to a whisper, and we're inching along. Over on the other side of the reef, the water is the color of Ming's nail polish. Out here it's a dark violet blue. The shipwreck is laying up against the reef on the deep side, that's what Mr. Miles says. I look but I can't see anything from the boat.

At last the anchor splashes and the chain rattles as it plays out through the hawse hole. When we drop the sails, we're about fifty yards off the reef in eighty feet of water. Mr. Miles makes an X on the chart. We can't anchor right over the wreck because we could end up smashed on the reef too. Palmyra is a clump of trees in the distance. According to the chart, it's maybe half a mile away.

The anchor is set, the boat is secured. Miss Marty watches us while Mr. Miles and Captain Dan rig up the gasoline generator and the air compressor to fill the scuba tanks. Now we're allowed to go swimming. The rest of the kids hurry to get their suits on, they dive off the side. Not me. I don't want to be in the water. I hate it. Ever since Lucas Marshall held me under in the deep end of the pool when I was six years old. I can still see his evil face under the water, bubbles coming out of his nose and mouth as he laughed.

If I wasn't such a wimp, this would be my chance. To swim to Palmyra, find one of the scientists, and beg for—what's the word?—amnesty. Or asylum? But I don't think I can swim that far. And there are sharks in the lagoon. But it's not the sharks I'm scared of.

I give them about ten minutes of splashy fun. I'm watching Steff and Ming in their colorful bathing suits, legs scissoring under the water, their hair swept back like seaweed. Bastien surface dives, his long body moves through the water. He's a seal, he's going to attack them. They pretend not to see him, but they know he's coming. It's Ming he preys on first, he comes up between her thighs. Now she's riding on his back, holding onto his neck. She's shrieking but not with fear. She wraps her legs around him and holds on as he takes her under. Steff is next. He grabs her legs and pulls her down and they're all underwater tangled up together. At last they pop up to the surface, gasping and laughing, and I can't stand it anymore.

"Shark!" I holler, pointing. "Shark off the starboard beam! It's huge, it's Jaws. Get out of the water!"

Like torpedoes they head for the boat, all arms and legs churning up the water. They scramble up the rope ladder hung over the side, they're shouting and laughing and pushing each other. Their sleek, dripping bodies are gorgeous. Even Truman, who waddles like a pudgy penguin in his too tight swim trunks, he's beautiful. They have swum in the ocean. They are different somehow, like they were reborn in the water. Only I am dry and hot and unchanged.

"Where's the shark?" Truman wants to know. "Was it a tiger shark or a reef shark? Black tipped or white?"

"I don't see it now. It's probably right underneath us. It was huge. I think it was a Great White." It's hard to keep a straight face. I'm glad I spoiled their fun.

"Really? You probably didn't see a shark at all, you just made that up." But his eyes are shining, he's thrilled to have swum in the Pacific Ocean with the dangerous sharks and the nearly naked girls. I am such a coward and everybody knows it. Ming gives me the cold shoulder, she won't even look at me.

One by one they rinse off under the deck shower—a big container filled with rainwater hoisted up on the mast. The wooden deck is wet with their footprints. The girls wrap their smooth bodies in bright striped beach towels and go up to the foredeck to comb out their hair. The Big Three show off their lean man-bodies by lounging against the stern rail. Salt crystals sparkle on their shoulders, their backs are bronzed and free of zits. They look like celebrities. This is their movie, it's all about them.

"Did you see a shark or not?" Truman needs to know. "Tell me the truth."

"I did. I think I did. But it might have been a shadow. Yeah, on second thought, I think it was a shadow."

"You little asshole." Bastien's voice. And now I'm down on the deck, face first, my head ringing. I taste my own blood and hear laughter, like seals barking.

"You ought to watch where you're going, Jimmy McCafferty. One hand for yourself and one for the boat, remember?" He offers me his hand, as if to help me up. It's a man's hand he offers. Big. His forearm is muscular, I can see the blue veins standing out. But I'm not falling for that old trick. I get up on my own, my head is spinning. I spit a mouthful of blood into the scuppers.

"What the hell was that for?"

"For being a crazy dickwad." He shows his big white teeth, but it's not a human smile. It's an animal baring its teeth. "You fuck with me again,

McCafferty, and I will crush your little peanuts and throw you over the side. Then you'll see some real sharks, little man."

And here comes our counselor getting into the action. But she doesn't say anything to Bastien, she starts scolding me instead. She's telling me the story about the boy who cried wolf.

"We all rely on each other. We're a team, James. We have to build trust, not destroy it. Honesty and communication, these are important values." Blah blah blah. She goes on in her cheery way. She doesn't see my swollen lip, my bruised nose, and I'm not going to tell her. I know something about being a team and that is you don't snitch. You take it like a man. You plan your revenge.

❦

Miss Marty volunteers to fix supper so that we can help Captain Dan and Mr. Miles prepare to go diving after dark. The shark incident is over, but I'm still on the outs. I'm a shadow they all avoid. I help Captain Dan launch the dinghy. Hopefully we won't need a lifeboat while they're using it. I help pass down the equipment: scuba tanks, wet suits, regulators, mesh bags, floats, and underwater flashlights.

"Traditional junk sailors wouldn't have had all of this gear," Miss Marty teases.

"We have to make a few concessions to modern technology. Besides," he adds with a superior smile, "the ancients were clever. They were resourceful. They might not have had compressed air and regulators, but they went underwater with hollow reeds to breathe."

He loves to show off his knowledge, and she pretends to be impressed. They give off a scent, like animals in season. They're getting ready to mate. I can feel the pull between them, strong as the tide.

What am I, some sort of radio? A receiver, an amplifier of signals? What's it like, I wonder, to be alone with your own thoughts? To feel nobody's emotions but your own?

❦

The dinghy is loaded and ready. We stop to watch the sun set. It looks like a big orange marble balanced on the edge of the world. For a second I think it's going to roll around the rim, but instead it sinks like a stone. The top slice of it turns vivid green as it disappears.

"Wow!" Miss Marty says. "Did you see that?"

Mr. Miles nods. "That was a green flash. You only see it under certain conditions. Some trick of optics. A green flash is a good omen."

"I've heard of them," she says. "And now, I've seen one. What an amazing phenomenon! Did you see it, James?"

I nod. I did see it. But I see optical tricks all the time. Right now flashes of emerald light leap from Miss Marty's head and heart and hands, but I seem to be the only one who sees that green flash.

⚎

Bastien gets to go with Captain Dan and Mr. Miles. He's a PADI-certified diver, he's got a card in his wallet to prove it. He's been diving in Cozumel and Costa Rica—he's the shit. And so Golden Boy gets to go night diving. Fuck him. I don't want to go down there anyway, I know what's waiting.

But Ming does. She wants to go, she wishes she was a certified diver. So does Steff. They think it sounds fun to sink down under the water, a big tank of air strapped to their backs. They want to put a regulator on and breathe out of a hose. They're both in love with Bastien, and my heart's a thirty-pound anchor.

The three of them climb down the side and get into the dinghy. They don't start the engine, they use the oars and row the boat to the reef's edge. It's not very far. Then one by one they roll off the side. One by one they disappear into the black water. We can see the dancing of their lights under the surface. They're down there a long time. Their bubbles rise, little beads of mercury in the starlight.

"What is it they're after?" Steff asks Miss Marty, who's watching through the night vision binoculars.

"Miles said they're hoping to find the wreckage of a supply plane that missed the runway."

But when at last they surface and we start hauling up the nets, it's not metal fuselage we're bringing in. It's an old piece of wood, shaped like a dragon's head and heavy as stone. Pieces of pottery covered with coral. A trunk, crusted shut with barnacles. Word flies around that they've found the missing Spanish treasure, but I don't believe it. These are artifacts of tragedy we're bringing aboard, and all I can think of is the ghosts they've disturbed. Ghosts who will gladly climb aboard to join all of the others below in the hold. Spirits who want what we have. The dead know gold is worthless, it's the treasure of breath they want.

⚓

Scorpio is high in the southern sky when at last they finish. The lifeboat is back on board now, the anchor winched up, the sails set. We don't put out our running lights, the lanterns with the colored glass, red and green. Not yet. They don't want anybody on Palmyra to see us leaving. This has been a black ops maneuver, top secret. I hear Captain Dan and Mr. Miles talking. Their voices drift up from below through the open port lights.

"This is really big, Dan. We have to be circumspect."

"The whole reef is off-limits. I don't want any trouble from the authorities."

"A five hundred year old wreck—we've got to get in on this. We discovered it. We have to get credit, to profit from it somehow. It's ours."

"Mark the coordinates. We'll come back later, just the two of us. Have us another look. Meanwhile we can do an analysis of the stuff we brought up. Might not be that old. There's no proof the Ming Chinese ever sailed this far into the Pacific. Not until much later."

"Sure looks like Chinese bronze coins to me. And the celadon bowl. What do you make of that?"

"Maybe you're right, Miles. Wouldn't that be something? We need to find us a billionaire to finance the project."

Both men laugh and I hear the clink of glasses. I dread to think what else they've brought aboard.

❧❧

There's no moon. The sky's black but the stars shine so hard they light our way. The Captain and his mate talk late into the night. Their voices hum and rattle the bones of the ship, which moves more slowly now because of the dead ones in the hold and the new ones, clinging like seaweed to the bottom of the ship, waiting for their chance at life.

❧❧

It's late, the incense stick is half way burned down. The wind sings in the rigging, the same three notes over and over. The tiller is lashed. We're sailing along on a broad reach, and if I don't allow myself to think of the future, it's actually quite nice. Bastien is sprawled out on the cockpit bench, sleeping. I nudge him, hearing Captain Dan's cabin door open and the sound of his footsteps approaching. Bastien jumps to life.

"Go below and sleep well, me hearties. You've earned a rest," the old man says to us. "Mr. Miles and Miss Marty will take the helm for the rest of the night. They'll be up on deck shortly."

Bastien goes below but I hang out on deck a little longer, pretending to watch for meteors. At the opposite rail, on the windward side, the first mate and the counselor stand shoulder to shoulder looking at the stars. The wind carries their words through my head.

"You'll have to come with us when we return," he says. "If you want to be in on the adventure."

"Oh Miles, I'd love that," she gushes. "I'd love to. Could I dive with you?"

"There's some theory to it you'll need to learn. Safety procedures. I'll teach you everything you need to know."

He reaches into his pocket. "Here, I've got something else for you. A little treasure, a souvenir from the deep."

I can't see what it is. He presses it into her hand and folds her fingers around it. A burst of pink and green light leaps from her hand, her heart, her head, like a volcanic eruption.

"Ooh, thank you! I'll treasure it always."

No! Throw it overboard, that's what I want to say. But I don't. I don't say anything because she wouldn't believe me. I'm tired of being the messenger. Let her find out for herself. I wish I would have been brave enough to escape when I had the chance. I could have been on the island by now. I'm such a coward and that'll be the death of me.

Chapter 13

It's our last watch together, Bastien and I. Tomorrow we draw new watches. I don't care who I'm paired with as long as it's not Bastien again. I'm pretty good now at the tiller, I can keep a course and I kind of like to steer the boat. I'm too young to have my driver's license, not for another year, but I can steer a boat in the middle of the Pacific Ocean, I can read a compass, and I can follow the stars. I feel good about that. I feel competent and in control.

Bastien falls asleep like he always does, and I'm alone with my thoughts. The ghosts know it and they want to come up to roam the deck like they do every night. But tonight at the top of the three masts, there's a strange blue light. It looks like the flickering blue at the base of a flame. Mr. Miles says it's called Saint Elmo's fire. It's some sort of electrical field, a phenomenon that occurs in certain atmospheric conditions, and it can distort the compass readings, its only danger. Saint Elmo, he says, is a nickname for Saint Erasmus, the patron saint of sailors. Does Saint Elmo work with Mazu, I wonder? Or maybe Saint Elmo and Mazu are one in the same, a god that can assume different forms. One thing I know is that flames keep the ghosts at bay. I'm nudging Bastien to wake him up. I want him to see Saint Elmo's fire flickering at the top of the masts. I want to hear his human voice. The ones inside my head are waking up now, grumbling and sighing.

"Hey, Bastien, you've got to see this. It looks like the masts are on fire. But they're not burning."

Nothing. He doesn't stir. I dare to touch his shoulder, a little nudge.

"You want a cup of coffee, bro? Some Skittles?" I reach deep in my pocket for the last pack I brought from home. Tear the top, take one and put it on my tongue. Bite down on it and YELLOW fills my mouth, a sweet-sour sugar rush.

"What I want, you little prick, is a good night's sleep. Set the self-steering. Put this piece of junk on autopilot and shut the fuck up."

"Why do you hate me?"

"I don't hate you, doof." He turns over on the hard, narrow bench, trying to get comfortable.

"Yeah, you do. You hate me. You despise me."

"Don't be all self-important, McCafferty. Why would I hate you? You're insignificant."

I pop another Skittle in my mouth. For courage. "Fuck you, Bastien." I say it out loud. Now he's probably going to get up and hit me, but instead he laughs. Not like a real ha-ha-ha laugh. More like a milk-through-the-nose snicker, which sends a feel-good rush of warmth through my body. With Bastien, this is as good as it gets. Instead of punching me, he snort laughed. I made him snort laugh. Think I can I do it again?

What is it about Bastien? Why do I want him to like me? The girls like him. Why is that? Steff's adoration for him lights up her face. And Ming, she pretends to scorn him but thinks he's hot. She wants him to notice her. I can feel her wanting him, like I want her, and I hate it. I hate him.

"So was your dad abusive? Did your mother abandon you? Were they meth addicts? Or did they just not give a shit about you?" I'm wondering aloud, but he doesn't hear me, or maybe he's already asleep again. I should just shut up, quit while I'm ahead. Never rouse a sleeping bear.

I want Bastien to like me. I want to please him. Does that mean I'm gay? Right now I wish he would give me a man hug, I want him to wrap those man arms of his around my chest and squeeze the breath out of me. I would do anything he asked, yes, even that, and I'm disgusted with myself. Push it away, deny it, that queerness. Shove it into the black hole where the dead men can do unspeakable things with it. I want to despise him. I have to. I want to make him look small in front of the others, I want him to fail. My hate for him is a little fire in the waste can that I'm feeding with scraps of whatever I can find.

It occurs to me I could hurt him, I could fuck him up right now, if I wanted to. Now, while he's sleeping. I could even kill him. If I had a weapon. When we sleep, we're most vulnerable. Bastien trusts me enough to fall asleep beside me. Or else he thinks I'm not capable of hurting him. I'm nothing more than a mosquito to him.

I put another piece of paper in the imaginary waste can and watch it flame up. But at the bottom of that fire is something valuable, something I need. If I could just reach in through the flame and rescue it, but I don't have a fireman's coat and gloves. Maybe it's safe, below the fire. I hope it's still alive. They say to get low if you're caught in a burning building. The heat, the flames, the dangerous gasses rise. The safe place to be is on the bottom.

I'm watching over my enemy while he sleeps on the cockpit bench. I'm responsible for his safety. It's up to me to keep the boat on its course. It's up to me to keep a lookout for storms and passing ships. I can protect him from the demons that roam this ship, the hungry ghosts that come up on deck at night. The flame in the lantern keeps them at arm's length. They're drawn to flame, yet repelled by it. I'm Bastien's protector but he doesn't know it. His long legs are bent up toward his chest, one arm under his head for a pillow, the other thrown over his face. I take off my hoodie and put it across his shoulders. The cold night air makes me shiver. It keeps me awake. What would it be like to pray, I wonder? What would I pray for?

⊲⊳

The trade winds weaken and die. We're following the equatorial belt, Mr. Miles says, to stay clear of a tropical storm forming off the coast of Mexico, a storm we heard about on the short wave radio, station WWV. Mr. Miles assures us that the narrow band of about five hundred miles on either side of the equator is a kind of safety zone out of the path of hurricanes and typhoons. He calls it the ITCZ, the Intertropical Convergence Zone. The winds here are shifty and unreliable, he warns.

It's raining—a cloud burst—the drops pelt us like BBs.

We collect the fresh water in anything we can—buckets, empty cans. The captain and first mate rig the sails to catch water for drinking and washing clothes. They're in their swim trunks, washing their white bellies and hairy underarms with slivers of soap, urging us to do the same. Only Miss Marty joins them. The three adults showering on deck, it's a hideous sight. The rest of us huddle below, hot and sweaty.

We're drifting in a westerly direction on one of the equatorial surface currents, Mr. Miles says. When we cross the equator into the southern hemisphere, we'll pick up the countercurrent, flowing eastward. Then we'll be inducted into Neptune's Society. Mr. Miles says it's a time-honored tradition in which newbie sailors crossing the equator for the first time pay homage to Neptune, the god of the deep. He won't tell us the details of the ceremony, but I'm worried that it will encourage the apparitions who are growing bolder by the day. I don't want any part of this, but where can I hide?

At night they are most active. You can hear them below, banging around, crying, howling. They've become cocky, maybe because of where we are, some kind of mid-Pacific portal or vortex, like the Bermuda Triangle. Actually, there are twelve known graveyards of the deep, twelve Devil's Triangles. I read about them in one of the books in ship's library. Mr. Miles says all of the disappearances associated with these ocean portals are coincidental, but I don't think he's read the book.

The sky looks troubled, a jumble of clouds. The wind heaves a sigh and then stops. A last breath. We haven't seen another ship or even heard a jet overhead for days. How many days? I have nothing to write in my journal. Except for the radio, which is ever more unreliable, we have no contact with the rest of the world. We have no proof that we are still in the twenty-first century.

⊰⊱

This evening we cross the line into the southern hemisphere. As the night deepens, Scorpio scuttles out from the underworld and spreads his stinger across the sky. Mr. Miles points out the Magellanic Clouds, a smeary blur of light to the south. If you look right at it, you can't really see it. Like a ghost, it's best seen out of the corner of your eye.

The moon rises, misshapen and dirty looking. It climbs quickly, disappearing behind a cloak of clouds. You can still see its light leaking around the edges. Captain Dan appears, carrying a trident and wearing a crown. Mr. Miles is his attendant, he is dressed like a pirate, shouting "Yo ho ho!" He blindfolds us all and asks us riddles we can't answer while King Neptune steers the vessel. We are made to scrub the deck on our hands and knees, blindfolded, using blocks of sandstone. "Arrrrgh, me hearties, yo ho ho!" One by one, we are lowered into the ocean in a canvas bosun's chair suspended on a boom tackle. One by one, we are baptized in the watery graveyard beneath us.

Do you know what "yo ho" means, James? It is what the corpse carriers chant as they carry dead bodies. They call out yo ho, yo ho! It came to your pirates by way of China, through the mouths of coolie sailors, from the ears of shanghaied sailors, taken aboard trading ships dead drunk, and when they awoke they were far out to sea and forced to work, were beaten with the lash if they didn't. Oh, James, you have led such a coddled life, like a young prince of the blood. You have no idea what you are in for. I must prepare you.

Yu is here beside me as my toes touch the water, he is so close to possessing me as my body plunges into the sea. I feel his arms and legs around me. He grabs onto me like a drowning boy, he is pulling me down. I'm starving for air. I'm choking on salt water and the pirate saves me, hauls me up, shivering and screaming. *Yo ho ho,* he laughs as he swings the boom over and returns me to the deck. Above, the clouds part and the moon shines down, and I see them crawling up from belowdecks, climbing over the side, crowding onto the deck, hundreds of them, faces half-decayed, like my father's, only he is not among them. He has gone missing, and I'm alone in this hungry crowd, all these dead people who want to be alive.

Don't be afraid of them. You are mine, Yu whispers tenderly, his words cold against my left ear. *I promise.* I feel his cold hand slide between my legs, groping for what he lost.

⌘

The other kids are on the foredeck, talking and laughing, excited from the dunking ceremony, drinking hot chocolate and eating marshmallows. Except for Truman, he's down at the nav station turning the dial of the old radio. He's searching for a signal. I can hear its squeal, like the sound effects from an old science fiction movie. Back in the cockpit, Miles and Miss Marty are kissing, I see their faces touch. King Neptune has stumbled to his stateroom to make love to a bottle. The moon is hidden behind clouds again. The ghosts are invisible, but I feel their presence, and below, just under the water, glowing balls of green, phosphorescent squid come up from the deep to feed. On what, I wonder? Spit into the water, a gob of mucous, my own DNA, and watch as one of the glowing forms pounces on it. I am doomed.

Chapter 14

Time goes by so slowly at sea. Each day is pretty much the same. Sometimes a seabird follows us, circling the boat. Curious, or maybe wanting a safe haven. One morning at sunrise there were two birds—black noddies—resting on the rail. I want to tame them, but they fly away.

Every once in a while, a pod of dolphins appears, and that's the highlight of the day. First you see the sleek gray humps of their backs as they swim near the surface in an up-and-down motion, like the waves themselves. Keep watching and you'll see them leap out of the water, you'll catch glimpses of their underbellies, a rosy color. Such strong swimmers and graceful as legless, armless ballerinas. We all love to watch the dolphins. It's the one thing that brings us together from every part of the boat, and we're always excused from any chore to watch them as they pass. Mr. Miles says the dolphins bring good fortune. I don't know about that, but they always leave me feeling a better person for having been among them, if only for a few minutes. They never stay very long, they have places to go and things to do. They just come by to tell us something important, or maybe just to race the boat. If I'm reincarnated, I'd like to be a dolphin.

Tomorrow the captain will choose somebody to give their report. I hope it's not me because I'm not ready. No way. Maybe instead of Chinese ghosts I'll report on dolphins. So much more cheerful. Everybody loves dolphins, they're like dogs. There's a book on the shelves about marine mammals. I'll see what I can find out.

⚜

The wind has died. The sails hang limp and the vessel sways from side to side as energy moves through the water in long swells. You'd think the ocean would be smooth if there isn't any wind, but it's not. It's restless, all the time. Maybe because of the tropical storm off the coast of Mexico, hundreds or thousands of miles away. Mr. Miles says it's been upgraded to a hurricane. A category two. Its name is Fausta. Fausta was a Roman empress, he says, and starts to tell us about the kind of ships the Romans used. Is there no escaping history? So much history. It's so heavy, I can't bear it. The present moment is an illusion. Grasp it, try to hold it, feel it, but it's gone, sucked into the black hole of the past.

⚜

Truman yawns and then I yawn. It's a yawning contest. Truman's my new watch mate. We've been on duty since four in the morning, the incense stick is nearly burned out. Soon we'll ring the bell and beat the drum, announcing the end of our watch. The sun has just come up and already it's hot. The sails start to swing and rattle as the junk bobs on the lumpy water. My stomach is churning again, like it did the first day at sea. Maybe Ming will put another scopolamine patch behind my ear.

"Welcome to the doldrums, me hearties," Mr. Miles says, coming up on deck in his bare feet. He has shaven and neatly braided his thin strands of hair, which stick out from beneath a clean bandana—red, not blue. He looks refreshed. The rolling of the boat doesn't bother him. "Let's drop the sails and lash the tiller. We're dead in the water."

"How long will this last? This stillness." I don't like it, not at all. We're not moving, not going anywhere, we're just being jostled around.

Mr. Miles scans the horizon. I'm wondering if his dark shades give him some sort of super vision. But he just shrugs. "Who knows? Could be hours.

Or days." The first mate launches into a lecture about the forces that affect the Pacific Ocean's wind patterns—uneven heating, Hadley cells, the Earth's rotation, high pressure and low pressure. His words are as hot as the air around us. Without a breeze to blow them away, they keep piling up and piling up.

"If there's no wind, why are we rolling around so much? Why isn't the water flat and still?"

"There's a lot of energy moving through the water. Like when you throw a stone into a pond, the ripples travel a long way. Somewhere the wind is blowing like stink." He shook his head. "But not here."

"It's freaking hot," I say, fighting a rising panic, trapped in the middle of all this blue. I miss the sense of motion, of going somewhere. I miss the wind on my face.

Someone strikes the breakfast gong. "Pancakes are ready!" Steff calls. "Come and get it, you sea dogs."

Good. Breakfast. Something to take my mind off of my misery.

"Gentlemen, mess is served. It's chow time. Let's eat," Mr. Miles says, lighting a new incense stick with his stainless steel pocket lighter, a vintage model, engraved with his initials. I feel my empty pocket, missing the weight of my lighter.

"Race you!" Truman, suddenly wide awake, charges for the companionway and I am quick on his heels, running across the rolling deck. We go bounding down the ladder and slide onto the bench, taking our normal places at the saloon table. The others come stumbling from their bunks, with sleepy faces and hair all matted together.

At sea you look forward to the smallest, most insignificant pleasures. Aboard *Good Fortune*, Sunday morning means pancakes, which are everyone's favorite treat. Especially Truman's. His eyes light up as he waits for the plate stacked high with thick, golden discs to come around to him. I envy the way he can forget everything else except what's in front of him. His ability to focus on a small part of the whole. I watch him spread a big hunk of butter on his pancake, he's careful to cover the entire surface. We have real butter on board, we keep it in the icebox. The big block of ice has mostly melted, but it's still cool inside.

I'm waiting for the syrup. It's in a big red can with a picture of a lion, it looks like motor oil. I make little butter eyes, nose, and mouth on my pancake face before I drown it in golden stickiness. Now to cut the face up into bite-size pieces.

Captain Dan and Mr. Miles come into the saloon to get their share of pancakes and a refill on coffee. We're all eating together before the morning muster. Pancakes and the last of the fresh Hawaiian pineapple, already brown in spots, and soft. The first signs of decay.

A big cross swell hits us, and everything on the saloon table jumps into the air as the boat seems to stop and then falls down the backside. We grab our plates to keep them from sliding.

Mr. Miles is standing up. He's next to the stove, he balances like a cat, like he knows it's coming. "Ha, don't you love those potholes?" He licks a drop of coffee that splashed out of his cup and onto his wrist. "Hey, where's our ship's counselor? I can't believe she'd be late for pancakes."

Blank faces, shrugs all around. Everybody is noshing.

"Ahoy, Miss Marty!" Mr. Miles calls out. "Hot cakes, baby! Better hurry up or I'm gonna eat your share!" There's no answer, just the rocking of the boat and the rattle of dishes in the cupboards.

"She's not in her bunk," says Ming. The curtains are open, the bed neatly made, all ship-shape, her night shirt folded neatly on the pillow.

"Maybe she's in the toilet," says Steff. "I mean, the head."

"Why don't you go look?" He points to Steff. His jaw muscle is working, but I don't think he's chewing. "Make sure she's all right."

Steff slides out of her place on the bench and disappears into the forward part of the vessel to the tiny, foul-smelling crapper we all share. We can hear her pounding on the door. "Miss Marty? Are you in there?" We hear the squeak of hinges as she opens the door. "Miss Marty's not in the head," she calls. Her voice is high-pitched and tight, it sounds like a violin string, slightly off key.

The ship stops rocking, becomes motionless. Time has stopped. No one breathes, no one moves. We're a photograph, frozen in the present. There is no past, no future. Just now.

The spell is broken. We breathe, the ship rolls, the plates slide across the table again. And the gong above the sink shimmers as it sways, the light dances off it. Time has become unstuck. Truman sticks another forkful of pancake into his mouth.

Captain Dan and Mr. Miles look at each other, and I see the thought pass between them. "Well don't just sit there. Find her!" Mr. Miles barks, leaping to his feet. "Search the damn ship. She's got to be here somewhere. People don't just disappear into thin air. Come on, let's find her!"

"Maybe she went below for more provisions." That's me, my voice sounds like a mouse squeaking. I feel sick.

"You check the food storage locker, Miles," says Captain Dan. "I'll check the other compartments." His chair scrapes against the deck as he pushes back from the table. Bastien, Colton, and Myer follow him.

Mr. Miles pulls open the floor hatch and scrambles below, calling her name. "Marty? Are you down here? Somebody find me a flashlight. Maybe something fell on her."

I scramble to the box where the flashlights are stowed.

"Make it quick! I need light down here!"

"But none of them work!"

"What the fuck? Bring me a lantern! I can't believe this. Marty! Marty, are you down here? Answer me, for God's sake!"

I'm lighting the lantern. I hear him down there, moving crates, sliding barrels, cursing. I take him the light, he shines it into the farthest corners. I see the faces of the dead, their mouths open in that final gasp for air. But no Miss Marty. Miss Marty is not down here.

"Maybe she went for a swim," Truman says.

"That doesn't sound like something she'd do," Mr. Miles says. "Not by herself. Not without telling anyone. You two were on watch last. Did you see her on deck at any time during the night?"

I look at Truman, he looks at me. "No." I did see a woman walking the deck, but it wasn't Miss Marty. It was one of them. At night they walk all over the ship, like they own it.

The others come back to the galley without Miss Marty. There's a pause, a big white space of silence. No motion, no sound. Then we're hit by another swell.

"When was the last time anybody saw her?" Mr. Miles asks.

I feel everyone's terror, a powerful surge. We can't remember. Last night?

"Look, people just don't vanish off of ships in the middle of the ocean. She must have fallen overboard. Come on, let's go," he shouts. "Man overboard! You know the drill."

We do. Only this time it's not a drill, it's for real. Hearts pounding, feet flying, we rush up on deck. But there's no one in the water to point to, and no one to throw the life preserver to. There's no wind to fill the sails, we can't turn the junk around. We're not moving. We can't move, we're just rocking back and forth as the energy from distant storms moves through the water. This is nothing like the man overboard drills we practiced.

Ming grips my arm. "James, do you sense anything?"

How can I tell her? It's not a sensing, it's a knowing. A heavy, certain dread. Yet in spite of that, in spite of knowing, I'm thinking about Ming's hand gripping my arm and the flood of warmth spreading though me. I wish she would never let go.

"What is it? Tell me!"

"The *shui gui*. I'm afraid one of them got her."

Ming's blue fingernails dig deeper, biting into my flesh. "Don't say that, James!"

"OK, she fell off the boat. And she's out there somewhere, treading water. She's waiting to be picked up. Is that what you want to hear?"

"We have to believe that. We can't give up hope."

"I'm calling a Mayday," the captain says, hurrying for the companionway. "Miles, what're the coordinates?"

Mr. Miles pulls the GPS out of his pocket, thumbs the buttons like he's playing a video game. "I don't know," he says, his voice strained. "I don't have a signal!"

Of course there's no signal, we're in the portal. Signals don't reach us here. Don't they know that?

The first mate walks back and forth, he keeps trying to pick up a satellite signal. It's useless. Captain Dan will have to make a guess, using the last notation on the chart. His guess might be miles off. They know this and they're scared. I feel their fear—it's a boiling madness, a blind terror that takes over their reason. Now Mr. Miles is scrambling to launch the dinghy.

"Give me a hand here. Help me lower the dinghy. I'm going to go find her!" But even with all of us helping, it seems to take a long time to get the dinghy, our lifeboat, into the water. We're losing precious minutes as we haul on the line attached to the pulley, the tackle that lifts the little wooden boat up off the deck. And once again I hear the dead men singing, *yo ho ho,* like some sort of Chinese work chant, to help us pull in unison.

As soon as the dinghy splashes into the water, Mr. Miles scrambles over the side and steps into it. He lowers the propeller into the water, pulls out the choke, and yanks the cord on the outboard engine. It coughs and wheezes. We stare stupidly. He curses and tries again. And again. At last it starts. Thank God, it fires up! Putta putta putta putta, he makes a circle around the *Good Fortune,* and then a wider circle. He's following a pattern, a search and rescue pattern. He soon disappears behind a smooth blue hill, and all we hear is the sputtering of the engine and the sound of his voice.

"Marty! Mar-teee! God dammit, answer me!" He throws off a dazzling light, like a solar flare. I catch a glimpse of an emerald flash as he disappears into the mist. *Good Fortune* is surrounded by a blanket of gray.

"Hey, he forgot the oars," says Steff, pointing to the cabin top where the paddles remain. "Mr. Miles! You forgot the oars!" she hollers.

"He doesn't need 'em," says Bastien. "He's got an engine. An engine is better than oars any day."

Down below we hear Captain Dan cursing the radio. Something's wrong, he can't get it to transmit. Truman's looking over the captain's shoulder. They're both fixated on the broken radio. I look at Ming, but she won't meet my eyes.

The captain orders us all to go back up on deck and keep a lookout, and we do. But there's not much to see. If Miss Marty were here she'd tell us to reapply sunscreen, that we can still get burned even though it's cloudy, and we can't see the sun. She'd urge us to drink more water. She'd remind us how marvelous it is to be here now and what an adventure this is. I want to believe that we'll find her, that she'll surface, dripping and laughing, and call for the ladder and a towel. "You guys better have saved me some pancakes!" Maybe this is a trick, a bad joke. Maybe it's a test of some kind. A team-building exercise.

And then I spy something floating at arm's reach, just off the port side of the vessel. It's a clear glass bottle, a vodka bottle.

"Grab the fishing net!"

Steff runs to the foredeck and returns with the long bamboo pole, net at the end. She leans over the rail and scoops it up, lays it on the deck. There's something inside, there's a message in the bottle.

"Stand back!" Bastien grabs the mallet, the one Mr. Miles killed the fish with. He busts the bottle open with one good crack and glass shards fly.

Steff picks up the paper, and with shaking hands she unrolls it.

Dear Miles,
I love this blue milieu
our valiant crew
and you…

Her signature is a flourish, a blossom, of purple ink. *Marty Bowers.* She's drawn two hearts, like a tattoo, below her name. An arrow pierces them.

Chapter 15

"Mayday, Mayday, Mayday." The captain has been trying to get through on the shortwave radio for hours, but no one answers his calls for help. His voice is growing scratchy and hoarse, the big fist that holds the microphone shakes. Now he's making a strange noise, he's barking like a seal. Oh, I think he's crying. I was wrong about Captain Dan. He's altogether human.

A thick haze has fallen around us. We can't see more than a few feet beyond the boat, and beneath us the sea is as impenetrable as the sky. Somebody rings the gong and blows the horn every few minutes. We stand a vigil, one at the bow and one at the stern, staring into the shroud of gray watching for Mr. Miles to reappear with Miss Marty. The boat rocks back and forth with a violent motion, like some huge invisible hand is trying to upset us.

The radio has been dismantled. It's in pieces on the chart table, a tangle of wires like intestines, glass tubes tinkling against one another like broken ribs as they roll back and forth with the tremors of the ship. But it's not the captain who is working on the radio, it's Truman. My heart lifts with a ridiculous burst of hope. It's Truman who will save us. The youngest of us, the boy with

Asperger's, the nose-picking genius who keeps an arsenal of weapons at home in his closet. He will fix the radio and send an SOS and we will be rescued.

I have to believe this, I have to make room for this belief in my head. I spread the word like a true believer. "Don't panic! Have heart! Truman will save us!"

The others gather to watch as Truman studies the components spread before him. "Don't disturb him," says Ming, as if Truman could possibly be distracted from the compelling collection of parts laid out on the table.

Night falls fast, but still no wind. No moon, either. And no stars. The haze thickens, so thick you can touch it.

⚓

Mr. Miles has not returned, it's been two days now. The junk is ablaze with lanterns so he can find his way home. I keep pretending to hope, but I knew when he left he was gone for good. I know where Mr. Miles and Miss Marty are. They're down below, their bodies are in the storage lockers. The *shui gui* have them, they're taking over their bodies, stealing their souls. It might be a long process. Who will be next?

⚓

We kids huddle together in the cockpit. We're exhausted keeping up this vigil. Our combined aura is a bonfire, it comforts us and keeps the ghosts at bay. We decide to leave the lanterns burning all night while we go below and sleep. Sleep is our escape, it's our ticket home.

⚓

At night I see their faces in the portholes, begging to come inside. I hear them tapping urgently against the hull. But when I go up on deck, I don't see anyone or anything.

"Ahoy! Who goes there?"

No answer. The water absorbs everything. There is no sound but the bang and rattle of the ship as some invisible force moves through it, shaking it. We are stuck in this time and this place. Every clock, every watch on this ship has stopped. We are in the eye of the portal. Captain Dan spends most of the time in his cabin. I smell cigarette smoke. I hope he doesn't fall asleep and set his bed on fire.

Is this where Yu drowned? Is he trying now to trade places with me? Is he going to rip out my soul? Will it hurt when I die, I wonder?

I try to summon my father. I speak his name aloud to conjure his presence, that always works. But not this time. He is someplace else, far from here. But Yu is close by, he whispers to me constantly, rambling on like a madman. I sing out loud, I try to drown him out, but some of the words filter through and bounce around inside my head.

I've been stripped of my maleness. My jewels were taken, but my heart is still a man's heart, and my courage does not come from the missing member.

I sing louder, "Row, row, row your boat, gently down the stream. Merrily, merrily, merrily, merrily life is but a dream."

<hr />

It's been three days since Miles disappeared. That's what Ming says. She keeps track of time. We don't sleep in our berths anymore. Too hot and too isolated. Instead we crash on the saloon settees and on the floor with our pillows. It looks like one big campout.

I wake to footsteps on the deck above. Someone is walking around up there. My skin tingles. The song returns, but this time the words are different. The words aren't English, yet I somehow understand. The men's voices—grunts, chanting in unison—they're working together, some sort of gruesome task.

I open my mouth for the sounds to come out, but Ming cups her hand over it, shushing me. Ming hears it too. She's trembling. We grip each other and hold close.

"Maybe it's one of us," she whispers. "Or maybe it's Mr. Miles. Maybe he's come back."

Minutes pass. It seems like a long time. The footsteps stop, and we hear the rustle of the sails, the slap of the halyard against the mast.

"Maybe it's the wind. The wind coming up," Ming says. Her breath is sour, like milk gone bad. She closes her eyes, rests her head against my shoulder. Fear is so exhausting. The pressure of her head, the soft sour whisper of her breath fill the hole inside me. I'm Ming's pillow while she sleeps, and that's enough. The mirror around her neck protects us both. We're safe, at least for the moment. For this one breath. You can live your whole life in a breath.

⊰⊱

The sun comes up, burning through the many layers of gray. One by one the others wake and stumble up onto the deck. All the rainwater turned to a hot fog. We can't see beyond the junk's rail, we are wrapped in wads of gray. Even the memory of wind is fading. We are stuck here, the world has stopped spinning.

Chapter 16

I jerk, falling. Suddenly awake. Wide awake. The other world breaks up and dissolves, the sounds fade away.

My head's an old-time jukebox. It stores voices and plays them randomly, like some ghost has dropped a coin in and pushed the buttons. I saw a jukebox once, a real one. An antique. I was with my father on a road trip. I don't remember what state, it was a long time ago. I was maybe six or seven years old. I remember seeing the records all lined up like plates in a rack. Dad explained to me how it worked and gave me a couple of quarters so I could see for myself. I think there must be grooves in my brain like those old records, just waiting for somebody, some thing, to drop the coin and push the button. The mechanical arm will select the record, and the diamond needle will bring the old voices and long-ago music to life.

We've given up watching for Mr. Miles to return. Now we're waiting for a military cargo plane, a C-130, or maybe a Coast Guard helicopter. It's like waiting for Christmas—so hard to contain ourselves, the hours pass so slowly. We strain our ears for the ring of jingle bells, the whomp whomp whomp whomp whomp of the Huey. Santa himself, dressed in red velvet and suspended on a tether, he's coming down to rescue us, one by one. Inside the chopper, Mr. Miles and Miss Marty will be wrapped in blankets and sipping hot cocoa. They will be singing *Sloop John B*. We'll all be saved. We will all be together again.

The boat lurches as another swell rolls beneath us, the unseen force shoves the boat, tipping it, causing the dishes to rattle in the cupboards.

Ming has reorganized the watches. The schedule has fallen apart since Miss Marty's disappearance. She's made up a chart of duties and posted it on the whiteboard in the galley. It's written in her confident hand, using red and green magic markers. So far, only Steff and I are following it. Steff opens four cans of Dinty Moore, dumps them into a pot on the stove top, and stirs the stew with a wooden spoon, heating it through. She dips out the first bowl for the captain, knocks on his cabin door.

"Captain Dan? Are you hungry? I've made some beef stew." Captain Dan doesn't answer so she leaves the bowl like an offering on the navigation table where he'll be sure to find it. But instead Bastien eats it, licking the bowl clean with his wide snail of a tongue.

<hr />

The day grows rancid, swelling like a tumor. The heat is an evil force, we have nothing to fight it with. We lie around like plague victims, waiting to draw our last breath. I fall asleep frequently like a—what's the word?—narcotic. Or narcoleptic? I'm dreaming of Miss Marty. She's back on board like nothing's happened, only she's dead. Her hair is seaweed, her fingertips have fallen off, and her face is half eaten away, but she doesn't seem to know it, and we're afraid to say anything. She says my father is coming any day now to join us. She smells like a dead starfish.

I wake up, nothing's changed, I fall back to sleep. Something is next to me. I can't see it, but I feel its presence. Now a cold hand across my face. I can't breathe, I can't move! Paralyzed! Somebody help me! An ocean fills my lungs, my heart's kicking, kicking, kicking, I'm drowning—No! I want to live! Bring me back!

And then it's gone, the pressure, the force, the dread—I turn on my side breathing great gulps of air. I can't be in this coffin-like bunk, buried alive. I slide to the floor, glad to be unlocked, able to move, glad to be breathing.

The others are sleeping soundly. I shake them, I shake them hard, shouting their names, terrified to be alone.

They wake up gasping, choking, mad for air, and look at me as if I'm the culprit. Like I'm the one who was stealing their life from them. Below, the slamming of hatches, the many compartments, like a draft through an empty house, sucking doors shut in its wake. Slam! Bam! Bam!

"It wasn't me." My voice, a whisper. "It wasn't me!" A hoarse squeak.

"Go back to sleep," Ming hisses.

⚓

The incense stick burned out sometime in the middle of the night when all of us were asleep. The captain must be passed out in his cabin, we haven't seen him in a long time. Ming says it's been almost forty-eight hours. She keeps a journal of the days. Ming says we've got to wake him up. He's got to pull himself together and get us rescued. We're standing outside the captain's door, we're gathering our courage, our group force.

Ming knocks on the door with her hard little pine-knot fist. "Captain Dan! Wake up!"

My captain does not answer. His lips are pale and still.

Now Steff pounds on the door with both her hands. "Captain Dan, we need you! Get up!"

My father does not feel my arm. He has no pulse nor will.

"Maybe he's not in there," I say. "Maybe he went with the others."

Ming puts her hand over my mouth and hisses, "Shut up, James. Got it?"

"Oh, he's in there all right," says Steff. "He's just like my father. When the going gets tough, they hide in a bottle and let the rest of the family deal with the shit raining down."

"OK. Let's do it. Let's bust the fucker down." It's Bastien who takes hold of the latch and leans into the door. "Come on, you guys, give me a hand." It's like in the movies, we are going to break the door down. Everybody throws themselves against the door.

Uhh! Again! Uhhhh! Again! Ahhhhh! Three times we hurl our bodies, slamming into one another, accomplishing nothing but hurting ourselves. It's so much harder than you would think, breaking into a room.

"What about the hinges?" Ming says to Truman. "Can't we remove the hinges and take off the door?"

"Duh! No. The hinges are on the inside. Captain Dan could get out by taking the hinges off, but we can't get in. But if I had a gun I could shoot the lock off. I'll bet Captain Dan has a gun in his room. A gun to ward off pirates."

Bastien goes on deck. He gets the axe out of the emergency locker, the shiny new axe with the price tag still on it. "Stand back!" And he's swinging it at the door like what's-his-name in that old Stephen King movie. Crack! Crack! Crack! It's thrilling to watch him wield the weapon. He is our war lord, his fury explodes the door. We minions follow him, spilling into the cabin, stopping at the foot of a magnificent bed—the wooden headboard, footboard, and posts carved into the shape of dragons, heads and lashing tails entwined. We have entered the dragon's lair, we have come to rescue our Captain Dan.

Chapter 17

Captain Dan is indeed in his bed. But he is quite dead.

There's no need to shake him or check for breathing or feel for a pulse. The captain looks like a figure in a wax museum, a likeness of himself. Except his skin is gray. His eyes are wide open, almost popping out of his head, but they look as hard as stones. They don't shine. His mouth is a dark cave, blue lips pulled back slightly, almost smiling. It looks like he remembered something important and wonderful, just as he was dying. Like the last word out of his mouth was "aha!"

You can feel Death. It hangs in the air, it shimmers like sun beams. I hold my breath as long as I can, and then I breathe it in—Death. I fill my lungs with the sweet stink.

Moving as one body, we back toward the door, driven by a backdraft, a nuclear wind of fear. What should we do? We don't know, we have no idea. Someone closes the door, and we retreat to the saloon, walking on tiptoes, not daring to speak. In the saloon we curl up next to each other like abandoned kittens, mewing and crying until we fall asleep side by side.

"We've got to get rid of it." That's Bastien talking. I don't know how long we've been awake, we're still lying on the floor. The ship is rocking us, but gently. It's raining. The rain drops drum on the deck above us, like nervous fingers.

"We should be collecting it. The rainwater," Ming says drowsily. "Like Mr. Miles taught us. We should put out buckets or rig the sails." But no one gets up to do it. Way too much work. We just want to lie here, side by side.

"People are going to think we killed him. They're going to think we killed them all." This is Steff talking. She's speaking to no one in particular.

"No," says Bastien. "Why would we kill them? It makes no sense."

"It might," says Steff.

Colton snorts and voices an original thought, the first I've heard from him. "What's our motive? To steal this rat-ass boat?"

"Actually there are no rats aboard this vessel, have you noticed?" This is me talking. "Not one. Don't you think that's strange?"

"No, dumbass. That's a good thing. I'm glad there's no rats. They're dirty. They carry disease," says Colton.

"The rats have fled. They got off in Honolulu, before we ever boarded," I say. They knew. Rats are the first to leave a sinking ship."

"You dumb shit. The ship isn't sinking. It can't sink," Bastien says, "because of the way the hull is constructed. Individual watertight compartments."

"Mr. Miles didn't say it couldn't sink, he just said it was harder to sink," says Truman.

"They said the same thing about the *Titanic*," I say, "that it couldn't sink."

"The *Titanic* hit an iceberg," mumbles Steff, "and it happened a long time ago."

"Look, we're not talking about sinking. We're talking about rescue," says Ming. "We're talking about what to do with—you know. The body."

"Maybe *Good Fortune* sank a long time ago. Centuries ago. And all the rats aboard drowned, along with all the people. And then it rose out of the water. It's a ghost ship. And it came for us, to bring us back to the place where it went down."

They're staring at me. I'm freaking them out.

"To exchange places with us?" Steff asks. She gets it. I nod, swallowing hard.

"Maybe we *did* do it," I blurt out. "Maybe we did kill them, killed all of them, against our will. Maybe we're under their power, the *shui gui*."

"Shut up you crazy little fuck," snarls Bastien, "before I stomp your head in."

"Stop it," says Ming, sitting up. "Don't talk like that, either of you. James, we did not kill anybody. Got it?" Her black eyes pierce mine. She squeezes my arm. "We are innocent."

"No one is innocent. They've chosen us. They want to take over our bodies. They want to live."

"Why us?" says Myer.

"Because our lives are worthless," says Steff, turning away. "We don't deserve to live and they know it."

"Speak for yourself, Steff," says Colton. "Maybe your life is worthless, but mine ain't."

"No, Steff." Ming grabs her limp arm and pulls her into a sitting position. Steff is like a rag doll. She sits but she's all slumped over.

"We deserve to live as much as anyone else," Ming says, gripping her arms. "We didn't kill the adults. Whatever happened, it wasn't our fault. None of us are to blame. Captain Dan had a heart attack, or a stroke. He died of natural causes. Miss Marty accidentally fell overboard, and Mr. Miles disappeared trying to find her. He got too far away and ran out of gas or something. Maybe he's still alive. Maybe he's been rescued and now they're coming for us."

Steff wants to believe this. She looks at Ming, her face twisting into a horrible grimace. Ming wraps her arms around Steff while she cries, a strangling sound.

"So what do we do?" Bastien says. For the first time, he's asking a question. "What the fuck do we do now?"

"We have to work together," Ming says calmly, releasing Steff from her embrace. "We figure out how to call for help. We figure out how to make this junk sail. We rescue our own damned selves."

But how? That's the question.

⁂

None of us know how to pray or we would, I'm sure. We would drop to our knees and speak in tongues, if we could. We would accept any salvation offered. The girls reach out for our hands, and we form a human chain. The surge, like a current, runs through our bodies, connecting us. But it can't last.

⁂

"It'll attract sharks."

"It'll be really heavy. And awkward. How do we even get it over the rail?"

"The hoist, maybe."

"But how?"

"We could cut it up," says Truman, picking his nose.

"No, that's sick," says Ming. "Depraved. We can't violate his body. We'll find a way. The halyard, maybe?"

"First of all we have to get it out of the cabin and up here on deck." Colton, for once, has a thought of his own.

"We have to have a ceremony," says Steff, "like a mass or a funeral service. When my Aunt Alice passed, there was a celebration of life. My cousins played her favorite music and there was a video."

"But we didn't know him. Captain Dan. Dan Hogan. Hardly at all."

My father's ashes, what became of them, I wonder? I don't remember a ceremony, a funeral service. "We have to have a ceremony for his spirit to be at peace," I say. "We have to have a ceremony for all three of them."

The girls discuss this.

"We could sing something. A song. Miss Marty would like that."

"How about a moment of silence?"

"We could all hold hands again. That's kind of like praying."

"No more holding hands," growls Bastien. "Come on guys. Let's get this thing done."

"Truman, do you have the radio back together?" Ming says.

"Yeah, but I don't know if we're transmitting. I can't tell. And we're not picking up anything. It's a piece of worthless shit."

"Call another Mayday," I say. "Somebody might hear us." The dead will hear us, I'm certain.

"I'll make an entry in the captain's log. We can all sign it. As witnesses. That way when we're rescued, it's documented what happened to us."

"She's right." For the first time Bastien he has agreed with someone, he is backing up Ming's decision. "But let's do this thing. Let's get it out of here. The stench is all over the goddamn boat. Let's throw it overboard."

"But what about sharks?"

"Who cares? He's dead. Let the sharks eat him."

Will there be maggots, I wonder? Maybe his face is already half eaten away. What if an arm or something snaps when we lift him, breaking off like a drumstick on a roast chicken? The whole boat is a slow cooker.

"His body has probably turned to stew," says Truman.

The boat rocks violently, like somebody's shaking it. Yet we're not sailing, we're dead in the water.

"Who's with me?" Bastien looks from face to face. Each of us nods in turn. "Well, then. Let's get 'er done."

❧

Together we go down the ladder's smooth wooden steps and back to the captain's cabin, all seven of us. The smell coming from the room is sweetly putrid, I have to mouth breathe to keep from gagging.

"Get a grip," says Ming. At first I think she means to toughen up, don't lose it, but then I realize she wants me to grab a fistful of bed sheet. We're going to wrap him up like a burrito in his own sheet.

He died in his underwear, I can't help but notice. Old man's underwear, Fruit of the Loom. Stretched out, worn thin, and stained yellow in the front. His fleshy belly looks like he's pregnant with twins, like he's ready to explode. I turn my head and gag, but nothing comes up.

"Wait!" Steff says, holding her nose. "Maybe we should take a picture of the body. To prove we didn't kill him. To show he died of natural causes. Except my phone's dead."

"So's mine. They're all dead."

"Did anybody bring a regular camera?"

Myer did, and he was glad for the excuse to leave the captain's cabin to get it. But the camera battery was dead too.

"The *shui gui*," I said. "They suck power from batteries. None of our flashlights work either."

"It's probably just the salt air," said Truman, though not very convincingly. "It's really corrosive."

"Doesn't matter," said Bastien. "A picture of a bloated dead man doesn't prove anything. Quit stalling. Let's get this done. Everybody grab a corner. Three, two, one, lift."

He farts when we pick him up, a long low whispering fart that smells like decay. We all laugh, an obscene sound. But it feels good to laugh, what a relief!

"Damn," Bastien grunts. "This fucker is heavy!"

Now we're screaming with laughter. We're united, we're a team, we're playing a party game. Bastien and Colton at the head, under the arms, Myer and I on the legs, the girls in the middle. Truman holds the door open. We shuffle along, bumping into each other. The ship rolls, causing us to stumble, our burden sways like a hammock, from starboard to port. We manage to keep from falling or dropping it, but the cabin door isn't wide enough to pass through side by side. We have to lower the corpse to the floor and drag it through the doorway.

We somehow drag it up the ladder, using ropes and the gang plank as a ramp. We slide it over to the portside rail. We're panting, our hearts are pounding, we stink of sweat.

"Now what?"

"We're supposed to say a mass," Steph says, "or some kind of service."

A trickle of foul brown liquid emerges from the sheet. We stare in disgust as it trickles leeward, a muddy river, toward the scuppers.

"Let's just get rid of it," Bastien says.

Inside the black hole the voices rumble and one sings out through my mouth. *"Exalt O shores and ring O bells, but I with mournful tread, walk the deck my captain lies, fallen cold and dead."*

Somebody giggles, I don't know why, and soon everybody is laughing again, even me. We're laughing so hard it feels like crying. We can't talk, we're gasping for breath, the tears rolling down our cheeks until at last we're empty.

"What if it doesn't sink?"

"Shut up and grab hold of the sheet." Bastien is talking to me, he wants me on his side of the sheet. Colton and Myer have one side, Bastien and I, the other. Truman and the girls stand back to give us more room to swing.

"Wait!" Truman has the brilliant idea to put a weight inside the sheet—an old cannonball he gets from one of the storage compartments where the captain and Mr. Miles kept their treasures.

The sun beats down through the thick layer of clouds, the heat and the swaying of the ship are unbearable.

"Hurry up. Let's do it."

With a three, two, one, we lift him up onto the rail and over, the sheet ripping from the strain. The cannonball and the corpse fall in two separate splashes. Horrified, we lean over the rail and see Captain Dan floating just beneath the surface, staring up at us, the torn sheet like a toga, tangled around him. A trickle of bubbles comes from his open mouth.

"Oh my God," whispers Steff, crossing herself.

"That's just trapped gas being released," Truman says. But the look on his face is one of horror.

We all lean against the rail and watch as our captain floats just beneath the surface, sinking ever so slowly, as if he's reluctant to leave us. A sob breaks free from Colton's chest.

"Shut up," says Bastien. "Shut up, or I'll throw you overboard with him."

Chapter 18

I like the way her thin lips move, the flash of tiny white teeth, her pink catlike tongue. Ming is talking, she's telling me something she thinks is important. She's telling me how the Polynesians sailed the Pacific Ocean centuries ago, navigating without instruments. She's telling me how the night sky was their chart, how they memorized the movements of the stars. I want to help her—not because I think it matters, but because I don't want her to lose hope. I want to protect her and that beautiful flame of hope, I want to be worthy, I want to protect her, like a man. I want my life to have meant something.

Ming estimates we're just south of the Equator. Maybe one degree, sixty nautical miles, south of the widest part, the Earth's bloated waist. Or maybe we're right on the Equator, or just slightly north. All of our watches have stopped. Our cell phones with their clocks and their built-in GPSs are completely dead. We can make a good guess about our latitude, but without knowing, the exact time we can't figure out our longitude. We're probably drifting westward on the equatorial current, which flows from east to west, she figures. Judging from Captain Dan's last logbook entry, she estimates our longitude to be 165 degrees. But that doesn't do us much good unless we can get the radio working and broadcast a Mayday.

Truman's bored with trying to fix the radio, he's building a catapult instead. He's found some wooden spars, some spare rope, and a cannonball to use as a counterweight. He's dying to launch some flaming bombs into the ocean. "It'll help the rescuers find us."

"That's what the flares are for, True," Ming says. "In the emergency locker. Remember what Mr. Miles told us? Only fire them when you can see your rescuer or if you have radio contact and are instructed to. Otherwise, they're completed wasted."

"We don't even know if those flares are any good. Nothing else on this boat seems to work. But with the catapult and a little kerosene, we can launch our own homemade flares, as many as we want, to attract attention. We can fire bombs all night long until somebody sees us—maybe a pilot flying overhead."

"Maybe he has a point," says Steff. "Remember the story Mr. Miles told us? How the Hawaiian voyaging canoe was rescued when the pilot of an airplane flying overhead happened to look down and see a flash of light?"

"The Hokule'a," I said. "I remember. It capsized in a storm and that surfer dude, Eddie Aikau, took his board and set off for shore to get help. 'Eddie would go.' That became a slogan on bumper stickers and stuff. But Eddie never came back. Never was found. The *shui gui* got Eddie too."

"Stop it, James," says Ming crossly. "We're not talking about Eddie, and I don't want to know about your *shui gui*. Now, let's look at the chart."

I look at the damp, creased paper spread out on the saloon table. It makes no sense to me, just swirls of blue and deeper blue. It gives me a headache to try to read the tiny numbers, the depth. Fathoms, such an unfathomable word. The geography of the deep, the blue watery hell where the *shui gui* wait, like prisoners, for the exchange.

Ming points with her chipped blue fingernail to where she has determined we are. "The Gilbert Islands are east of us, I'm pretty sure. And Banaba Island is to the west." She takes the Pacific atlas off the shelf and finds Banaba. Her tiny little finger slides down the page as she reads. "They used to mine phosphate on Banaba. It was called Ocean Island until 1979. More than three hundred people live on Banaba, according to the 2005 census. So if we pass by closely enough, maybe we can get their attention with Truman's catapult. It's worth a try."

Steff nods, looking to Bastien for his approval, but Bastien is sprawled on the settee, asleep. Colton and Myer are in their bunks, they've given in to exhaustion. That's when you're most vulnerable. That's when the *shui gui* can get you. When you're sleeping.

"But right now, while it's daylight, we can try to signal with a mirror. I have a mirror, right here on my pendant. Do you know Morse code, True? It must be in one of these books. We can signal S-O-S."

"Yeah, it's in the ham radio manual. It stands for Save Our Ship," says Truman. "It's the only nine element signal in Morse code. Three shorts, three longs, three shorts. Dit dit dit. Dah dah dah. Dit dit dit."

Ming holds her pendant up to reflect the sunlight, but the sun is hidden behind the clouds. We can't see its yellow face, we can only feel its stifling heat. Right now we need rain and wind more than we need sun.

Truman is bored with signaling. He wants to construct a catapult and make bombs.

❖

There's no more water, there's nothing to drink. We've drunk all the soft drinks. All the canned lemonade and orange drink. All the fruit juice. No one kept track, we just sucked it down whenever we felt like it, tossing the empty cans down into the food storage locker. At night I hear the cans rattling, like a wind is blowing through there, but Ming says it's just the rocking of the boat. We've set out buckets, barrels, and washtubs to collect rainwater. Everyone has his own container, his own private water supply. I hope it rains soon. Ming says we can only live a couple of days without water. She has devised a water condenser, but so far only a few drops have collected on the underside of the plastic.

Bastien has moved into the first mate's cabin, he's taken over Mr. Miles's room, made it into his own lair. He drinks his liquor, smokes his cigarettes. He's got Steff in there with him, they spend hours and hours behind the locked door. I know what they're doing. We all know what they're doing. He doesn't let any of us come in. He's got his guard dogs to protect him. Colton and Myer lie outside the door, waiting for Bastien to command them.

Nobody sleeps in the captain's cabin, it still stinks of death. An imprint of Captain Dan remains on the mattress, the outline of his body, like police markings at a crime scene. His ghost is hanging around, and only one thing will send it on its way. I have to burn an incense stick and a candle to light the way for him. I have to burn hell money—the fake money Chinese burn for their ancestors to use in the spirit world. I don't have any, but there's a Monopoly game in the saloon.

The Monopoly money is different colors: white, blue, yellow, green, tan, and orange. I take all of the biggest ones, the five-hundred-dollar bills, and stack them carefully in a frying pan, putting all the tokens—the thimble, the shoe, the dog, the hat, and the ship—on top. Then I burn them in the captain's room, setting the pan on his mattress in the heart center of his outline and igniting it with a butane stove lighter. The stack of bills crackles as it blazes up, melting the little playing pieces into silver lumps that look like old teeth fillings. The smell of burning paper and lighter fluid covers the smell of decay. Next I lash some of Captain Dan's empty booze bottles together into a sort of raft, using pieces of twine I found in the galley. I stick more of the Monopoly money under the twine. I make a mast and a sail with a wooden spoon and a paper towel, tie a string around the whole thing. Light it on fire, lower it into the ocean, and cut the string. My version of the lantern ceremony. I want the spirits of Captain Dan and Mr. Miles to be happy and find their way. I was wrong about them. They were ordinary men. Just men. Not evil.

Bastien and his guards burst in, pushing me aside, nearly trampling me in their pillage. They ransack Captain Dan's room, pulling his drawers out, emptying his locker, rooting through his personal effects. They rifle through his clothes, flinging tee shirts and underwear out of the way as they look for the good stuff. And they find it, they find his stash of booze. They also discover a plastic bag filled with prescription pain relievers—Oxycodone and shit. They find the captain's protection, his handgun, hidden in a sock. They take their loot over to Bastien's cabin. Bastien gives Colton and Myer a bottle of scotch to share. They sit outside his door, guzzling it like water and laughing like goons.

⁂

Ming is sleeping, sprawled on the settee, dirty now. Her legs twitch, like a dog dreaming. The bottoms of her bare feet are black. None of us bathe anymore or wash our clothes. We are like a pack of wolves, snarling and baring our teeth at each other. We are unraveling. Disintegrating.

⁂

At night faces appear at the portholes, fingers scratch at the hull. They all want a piece of us but the ghosts already aboard won't let them on. They're waiting until we drift over the place where they went down. We must be getting close because they're getting bolder. They walk the deck even during the daylight now, dressed in their long flowing robes. Our worlds overlap. Yu doesn't say much, but he's nearby. He's waiting.

⁂

No wind. The air is still as death, but the energy from distant storms moves through the ocean, rocking us violently, shaking the dishes in the cabinets and tossing books off the shelves. We are the rag, the bone, clenched in the dog's teeth. The spirits are driving us out of our minds so it will be that much easier to move into our bodies. But I can't let that happen. I will stay sane. I must.

Bastien appears in a red silk robe. Where did he get that? Is he Bastien or is he one of them? The god in the red silk robe demands something to drink. He staggers, he roars—but the alcohol hasn't quenched his mighty thirst. I bring him a cup of my own urine, golden brown and as strong smelling as alcohol. His concubine has passed out from the narcotic pills, she is sprawled naked in his bed. I catch a glimpse of her white ass, her tattooed arm. He drinks my piss like he's doing a shot of whiskey, and then laughs and demands more. But I know urine won't keep us alive. Tonight is the fifteenth night of the seventh lunar moon, the Night of the Hungry Ghost. The gates of hell are opening, the full moon rises, there's no place to hide.

Fruit in cans, whispers Yu. *Mandarin oranges, pineapple, pears. Drink the juice and live. You must do it. Do it for me. Please James?*

Not for Yu, but for Ming. I will find water to keep Ming alive. If Ming lives, we all have a chance.

⌗

Armed with a can opener and a lantern, I creep down into the hold below the galley. It's dark, hot, and stuffy. I'm pulling the lids off of wooden crates and barrels, only to find them empty. Humming to fill my head so I can't hear all the voices crying and moaning for life. Where's the fruit cocktail? The canned peaches and pears? I'm dying to drink the juice.

I step on something. What's this? My lighter, it's my lighter. I've found my lighter, the one I lost a few weeks ago. Or was it only days ago? But what luck! My father's lighter, his initials engraved on the side. I can feel them with my thumb. It gives me a sense of peace, knowing he's near. I press the wheel that makes the spark and the perfect little flame jumps up. If only it was a fountain instead. A lighter that made water, fresh cool water.

Oh, what's this ahead, a door? An entrance to an adjoining compartment? I never saw this before. It must lead into one of the storage spaces where the salvage is kept. I can hear something on the other side of the door. It sounds like somebody's moving something heavy.

"Truman? Is that you?" No answer. "Colton? Myer?"

The door doesn't open. It feels like there's something behind it, keeping it shut. I set the lantern down and push the door while turning the handle at the same time. Huhhhh! Throw my whole body against it. Huhhhhh! The door flies open and I go crashing in, falling to the deck. I hit my head. My ears are ringing. Losing it, going under.

"Who's in here? Truman? Truman, is that you?" My head is pounding, my leg is twisted under me somehow. I can't move. Truman doesn't answer. It's not Truman. The light from the lantern flickers on the deckhead above me. If only I could stand up, or even get to my hands and knees. Nearby, a rustling, a scuttling near my ear. Sounds like a roach or a centipede. It must be huge. It's crawling on my neck, a hundred legs on my skin, seeking darkness in my ear or up my nose. It's going to feast on my brain. My heart is so big it's going to burst. It's going to explode in my chest, but I don't want to die, no, not yet. Don't give up, don't give in.

The boat rolls on a swell, swaying back and forth like a drunk woman. Barrels slide, crates topple, and behind me the door bangs shut. Darkness! Pitch black! Something heavy is crushing me, pressing me down. I'm trapped! Lungs busting! Help me, somebody help me!

Breathe easy, James. Don't panic.

Grope for my pocket, need the lighter.

I've told you not to play with fire. How many times have I told you not to play with fire?

Dad? Is that you? Are you here?

Don't play with fire, James. And don't ever smoke. I catch you smoking, I'll kick your ass.

It's not him. It's just a residual, an echo, bouncing around the universe. It's found me again, out here in the middle of the ocean. Fire seeks water to quench its thirst, to sooth it, to extinguish it. I remember the storm that long ago night. Crashing thunder, white flashes lighting up the darkness like a strobe light. I was scared, like a cat, the little hairs on my arms were standing straight up, and all I wanted to do was run and hide. I tried to wake you, but I couldn't. You were passed out. Then I saw your cigarette lighter on the floor, it had fallen out of your pants pocket. Maybe the lightning did cause the fire, like the newspaper said, but it might have been me, and I'm sorry Dad, I'm sorry, I got out, I ran outside and left you in there. They said you were dead from the smoke before the flames ever touched you. Paper, rock, scissors. Earth, fire, water. Water covers most of the planet. Now it will cover me.

⊰⊱

Something is burning, smoldering, exotic and spicy, something precious. Incense? The feel of fine silk, cool against my skin. Silk, the living thread of a thousand worms. The glittering eyes of the dragon watching over me, I feel them on my face, hot stones. The sound of a bird chirping, longing to be free of its cage. The chill wind makes the curtains billow like a sail and blows away the remnants of the dream. Her hand cups my chin, her finger presses against my lips. I ache with the gnawing hunger of a ghost tiger, a tiger stripped of his teeth, his claws. A white tiger, whose stripes are gone, and only the echo of his roar remains. I am invisible. I am Yu.

I was your age when I died, James. Now we are about to trade places, you and I. You becoming Yu. Poor Yu, the eunuch. Poor, dead Yu. And I becoming James, the lucky, living James, his whole life before him. How long I have waited for this day! Be still and know your past so that you may endure your hell, and I may be free of it. Listen, and I will tell you your story.

It begins over seven hundred years ago in the Middle Kingdom, the land you call China. An ancient land where human life is held cheap, where wicked spirits, capricious demons, and jealous gods rule through their chosen ones. You must know this to make sense of your terrible fate.

Chapter 1

Your name was Yu Chin; you were a eunuch. You served the emperor in his palace. You had been cut rather late, cut by your own father who sold you to the court in the summer of your eighth year.

I try to call out to the others, but his hand covers my mouth.

Quiet please! You'll alarm the others.

What was it like? The cutting? Of course you want to know. Your father was like the Old Testament Abraham, that blindly obedient man who held the knife over his young son's body. But no angel stilled your father's hand; no God called out from the clouds to let you go. Instead, your father used his blade like a farmer gelding his young hogs. Experience the terror, feel the pain, know your shame.

A burning pain sears my groin, I try to move, but Yu holds me down. I try to faint, to move to a deeper place in my mind, but he blocks my path, he forces me to listen. To watch.

Your male member, your little magic wand and your jewel sack, no bigger than a walnut, were severed from your body in two swift cuts. But the reason you were neutered was so that you could serve the emperor without ever being a threat to his lineage. You could not impregnate his women. You would have no lineage of your own.

You were the youngest of seven children. Your family, like most families in China, was poor; every day was a struggle to survive. Your parents thought they were doing you a favor, for a eunuch serving the emperor never wants for food. It's true, you never went hungry, and you always wore fine clothes. But for the rest of your short life, you had an angry red scar, like a crooked grin, where your penis and scrotum had been.

Your mother cried, it must be remembered, but did nothing to help you. It was your fate to be sold into the service of the emperor.

⸙

In your early years at the palace, before Lotus came along, Pau was your only friend. You and Pau became close during your days as initiates, living in the monastery, learning Buddha's teachings, the mysteries of the Tao, and the Emperor's laws. Although you learned to read—basic literacy was necessary to carry out your assigned tasks—you were not taught to think critically, to ponder abstract ideas, to study the sciences. The scholars did not want the eunuchs to have the power of knowledge. They did not want you to be able to manipulate words, those powerful tools that so easily can become weapons in the wrong hands.

In those years there were many eunuchs working in the Imperial palace, and their numbers would multiply greatly in the years to come. Many of the intellectuals resented your growing influence. Actually, they feared you. Do you know why, James? It's because all men fear emasculation.

There were many eunuchs; you were a class in and of yourselves. The eunuchs were the laborers, bodyguards to the harem, and confidants of the palace women. They served as officers in the army, the navy; they were the palace guards. Interesting that James's people enslaved a different race, the Africans, while Yu's people enslaved their own kind. Eventually, the eunuchs became so numerous they threatened the ruling class. But that was later, after Yu's time.

You and Pau were educated by the monks in the palace temple and in return you served the monks and the scholars as errand boys and personal servants. You learned to be good subjects of the emperor. You learned to obey.

Except you were not a good subject. You did not obey. Only pretended to while everyone else found purpose and order in the emperor's laws and in Fate itself. In the grand wheel of fortune, humans are but cogs.

But you were a ghost of a man, even while you were alive, a hungry shade who longed for what he could never have. You burned down a palace. You would have set the world on fire to save her.

Now I will have my chance to live in your world, James. In *your* body. I will be a whole man, a free man. And you? You, James, shall know what it's like to be me.

Yu seems to drift off, dozing like an old man. I try to escape now, but as soon as I try to move, he wakens and paralyzes me again.

Now, where was I? Oh, yes. Pau was a comfort to you in those days. You found solace in each other's quiet company. You licked each other's wounds like orphaned wolf pups. Though you were very different, you complemented each other.

Your friend had an amazing gift, a dexterity with mathematics. Pau juggled numbers like balls, and he could command them to do all sorts of tricks, though we had never been taught anything beyond very basic arithmetic. Numbers were like people to Pau, like friends and relatives. He knew the relationships they shared; he was privy to their intimacies, their love affairs and quarrels. While you were still in training, the emperor's advisors employed Pau to cipher for them. His gift for mathematics was inborn, his intuitive understanding made them look like amateurs. Yet they weren't jealous of him, for he was just a neutered boy. He was like a palace pet, he did tricks for them on command, loyal and guileless as a dog. They sent him on errands because he would see they weren't cheated. He went to the market for them, he went to the riverfront. He had a long leash and everyone liked him.

You didn't have your friend's capacity for numbers, but you were clever in other ways. While Pau could manipulate numbers, you could manipulate people. You developed the black art of deception and ruse. Your one true power was the ability to become invisible. It's easy, really, to be unseen. The great majority of people are invisible much of the time, and they neither know it, nor care. I'll let you ponder on that for eternity, my friend.

After training, Pau was employed as a scribe in the Ministry of Records, where he served the administrators, who recorded and filed the official papers. His talents were wasted there, but that is true for many, if not most of us, I suppose. Whatever age we live in, the most beautiful flowers are used as toilet paper for the mighty. The best of our poets are illiterate night soil collectors. Wisdom is burned to heat the wealthy man's palace. Beauty and kindness die with the girl abandoned by the side of the road. So few of us are able to follow our true paths.

Pau had a magnificent mind. He could glance at a manuscript and memorize it—even though he didn't comprehend the words. His job was to make copies, which he could do faster than anyone. Because he was so efficient, he was often sent on other errands. He was a runner and a procurer for the men he served. His superiors used him as an abacus, a copy machine, a handcart. He was their clever pet, a useful curiosity to enhance their own positions.

You were assigned to serve the emperor's concubines, a job given to the most effeminate of us. Unlike Pau, you had no useful gift, no great memory or facility with numbers, and you weren't aggressive or obedient enough to be a warrior, so you were given the default position as companion and protector of the palace women. You didn't like your assignment. That is, until Lotus arrived.

Lotus?

Yes, I knew you would be interested in her. Lotus was the beautiful flower in your life, and just as short-lived. You must know her as I did so that when the exchange is complete—when I become James and James becomes Yu—the memory of love will console you, deep on the dark ocean floor.

Like a prisoner who becomes attached to his tormentor, I know I am dependent on Yu. In a sick way, I admire him. He holds me down. He's going to kill me, yet I don't want him to be harmed. Why? Because he is so considerate of me.

Chapter 2

Good boy, James. You are no longer struggling so hard to escape. I've captured your attention. You want to know more. Well, I shall tell you.

Lotus was your good fortune and also your undoing. You were given the responsibility of watching over one slender thirteen-year-old girl named after a flower—the emperor's youngest blossom. Lotus, with the smooth, creamy skin and the fragrant hair. Lotus, with the exquisitely tiny, useless feet, bound at a very early age, deforming the malleable young bones. Small, crippled feet stirred men's lustful urges, made their penises erect as soldiers.

Why, you ask? I see it disgusts you, the shrunken, twisted feet. I think it was because women were made helpless by the deformity; like wounded animals, they were unable to run away. Crippled, they couldn't run; they could barely walk. They waddled, swaying back and forth on their tiny feet, which grew red and swollen from the effort. Even their swaying gait was seductive.

Only a rich man could afford wives with bound feet because these women could do no heavy work. They needed servants for that. A rich man's women were simply receptacles for his seed. Like beautiful ceramic vases. Girls with bound feet were very proud of them because it increased their worth. But not Lotus; she had a mind of her own. Her feet may have been bound but not her spirit.

When she was thirteen, Lotus was brought to the palace. She was nubile, on the cusp of womanhood, but small for her age. Her feet, those curled up, unopened buds, were her best asset; they were the tiniest feet in the Imperial City. Lotus was born far away in the hills, like some rare, exquisite orchid. Her parents died when she was very young. She was raised by her brother, who sold her to the court as soon as she came of age.

Her brother was a simple farmer, but he had his connections. He paid to have his prize flower presented to the right administrator, and his timing was perfect. By obtaining a new concubine, one so small and with beautifully erotic feet, the old emperor was announcing that he was still virile, still powerful, still a force in this life. Her presence was a compliment to him, the Son of Heaven, ruler of the Middle Kingdom.

But of course everyone knew the emperor was dying, even then. The concubines had been mere companions for the past year, little more than foot warmers, personal nursemaids who shared the old man's bed for the night, chastely rubbing his feet and aching back, while making the shrieks and moans of lovemaking to fool anyone who might be pressing their ear to the door.

For a long time none of the women would admit this for fear of disgrace, for fear of losing their imagined place, for fear of being dismissed, sent back to their village in humiliation. But one by one they whispered the truth to their closest attendant, the castrated man who served and protected them. Eunuchs gossiped even more than the bored concubines did, so the secret was out.

Lotus was a naïve young virgin when she first arrived, uninitiated in the rites of love. Part of your duty was to teach her what the emperor would require. As a eunuch you could not impregnate her. Your magic wand and jewels had been taken so that you, like the other palace eunuchs, would not be a threat to the emperor's women, whose bodies were receptacles for his seed alone. What man cares if two women pet and kiss one another? In fact, most men find that arousing. Likewise, the emperor was not jealous of eunuchs kissing and fondling his concubines. It was expected of them.

Your intimacy developed very gradually, for she was very private, very shy. It took many weeks of gentle coaxing just to be allowed to interlace your fingers with hers. Even though your male treasures had been stolen, stripped away, their ghost forms remained. Touching Lotus thrilled you. But you had to work to win her confidence. You had to prove yourself worthy. Lotus was not a frivolous girl.

Months went by before she allowed you to touch her budding breasts, first with your fingertip, and then with your hands cupping them, and squeezing. "This is what he'll want to do, Lotus. And you must turn your head to the side and sigh and make a little moan of pleasure."

One night she allowed you to slide your eager hand down the valley of her stomach to the mound of soft, damp hair and the secret place between her legs. What joy, what pain! Although you had been emasculated, you still had yearnings, like any young man. Yet you had no wand to become erect—there was only a scarred opening in your body for the urine to rush out when you removed the plug of wax. Just the angry red scar where a scrotum had once budded.

At fifteen years of age, you had the same smooth face, the delicate throat and hands, the same dreamy eyes and feathery lashes. You sprouted only a few stray hairs in the scarred landscape between your legs. Your heart became a brittle shell enclosing an empty nest, robbed of its eggs. A nest waiting to burst into flames.

You were one of the man-made humans, a separate class, a cruel design thought up and carried out by desperate men, to make certain they and their line would remain in power, to insure their heirs really were products of their own seed. This crime had become embedded in your culture and no one gave it much thought—as long as their own testicles were intact.

I feel you struggling to reach between your legs, James. James-becoming-Yu. But I can't let you move, nor speak. The transformation is not yet complete. Trust me, you will eventually get used to the emptiness there. Well, no. That is a lie.

Yu cries. I can't help but feel sorry for him.

⊨⊨

Yu became Lotus's best friend, her only friend. The consorts were very jealous of one another, especially of the youngest, the most fair. The one with the smallest feet. You wanted to be a man in full, but if you had been normal—uncut—you never would have met her. Your lives never would have crossed. You can't imagine life without her, yet you could never know physical love the way it's meant to be known.

You think you have it hard, as James. You think because your father died and your mother sends you away every summer, you are cruelly used. You suffer so because you think you caused his death, setting the house on fire. Oh, I know all about you, James. And now you are learning all about me. Be still, James. It's pointless to struggle. This is a dream, all a bad dream from which you will never awake. I'm sorry James, but it is our destiny.

⋇

As Lotus's guardian you had to monitor everything about her person: what she ate and drank, what time she got up and went to bed, how well she slept, and what she dreamed about. You were charged with making certain she attended her classes—music lessons, calligraphy, poetry—and went to the temple with the other concubines for spiritual lessons. It was your job to take her for walks in the palace gardens, and if she needed something beyond the walls, it was your duty to go get it for her. If she had a headache or a sore throat, you were duty bound to report that to the court physician. You even had to give him a detailed report of the onset and duration of her monthly flow of blood, which had only just begun earlier that year, at the beginning of the dragon moon. You were her chaperone, her guardian and nurse, and her servant too—for you couldn't deny her anything.

She loved for you to take her outside. You carried her through the palace gardens, down by the water where the birds splashed. Although she could walk, it was a tottering gait on those little stubs of feet. She liked you to carry her on your back, as if you were a horse and she, the warrior woman. That's what you played. Sometimes Pau joined in your childish games. The three of you, pretending you were an army, chasing the invaders, pelting them with arrows, driving them back across the wall. Lotus made it all come alive, the way she described the things she saw in her mind.

But in the evening when it was time for her bath, she was no longer the general-at-arms but became the woman, armed with softer weapons as she prepared herself for the emperor's bed. That was her duty. Her maid poured scented water into a bowl, releasing a fragrance of lotus blossoms, the flower for which she was named. You stood by the door, your back turned while she undressed. Your job was to ensure she was not disturbed or molested as she bathed. You heard the rustle of silk as her gown fell to the floor. The murmurs of girlish voices, she and her maid talking about womanly concerns. You heard the trickle of water squeezed from the sponge, a sound like rain running off the roof, and you felt a hunger in your soul that could have no satisfaction, no resolution.

Later, when the maid had been dismissed and you were alone at last, Lotus kissed your eyelids, the tip of your nose, covered your trembling mouth with her own. Her breath was warm on your face, and you came alive under her touch. Yet you hated your deformed body. An unseen fire smoldered inside you, a fire that could never blaze. Your male member existed only in your mind.

"You are my protector, Yu. My one and only true friend until death." She kissed you again, more fully, her slim hot tongue doing playful battle with yours. Your hands found their way into the slits in her night robe, like an animal seeking what it knows, blindly.

That arouses you, does it not James? Oh, I can't wait to be you, living inside your young man's body.

⋈

Every day Lotus and the other young women were schooled by their teachers, most of whom were virtuous widows of palace scholars. They learned to read, to play the lute or the flute-like sheng, an ancient instrument of our people. The wives, concubines, and daughters learned the basics of calligraphy, poetry, music, and painting—all of the arts. The emperor wanted his women and children to be cultured, to appreciate beauty and to be able to discuss ideas with him, to be aware of the vast knowledge and achievements of China—a great and old civilization.

So much older than yours, James. Can you appreciate that? More than a thousand years before your Jesus of Nazareth was born, China flourished under the Shang Dynasty. Followed by the Zhou Dynasty, which Confucius, our great teacher and philosopher who lived five hundred years before Christ, called a Golden Age. It was our Confucius who wrote a version of the Golden Rule. That is, *Do not do unto others what you would not want done to yourself.* A negative version of your Golden Rule.

China's history is long and her civilization rich. You were always eager to learn. Lotus brought books back from her lessons, she brought them back to her quarters and shared them with you. Lying side by side on her bed, bare feet touching, you read them together. What you remember most was the smell of her hair, her skin, her breath—and her concentration. Books were a way for her to escape the palace. The only way.

Poetry was her favorite; you loved to hear her recite in her murmuring, melodious voice. So poignant. You wrote poems together, in the style of Bai Juyi, a classical poet from the Tang period, five hundred years earlier. His words were like spirits, reaching across time to sweetly burn your souls. You discovered the poetess Li Ch'ing Chao, of the Song Dynasty, and drenched yourselves in the imagery of her poems. *In my narrow room, I throw wide the window, and let in the profound lasciviousness of Spring.* That's from her poem, "Mist." Is it not intense? Is it not exquisite? It finishes like this: *O bright pods of the pepper plant, you do not need to bow and beg pardon. I know you cannot hold back the passing day.*

Oh, James, it saddens me that you don't appreciate poetry the way I do. But when I am James, that will change.

The monks had taught you to read, but it was Lotus who taught you to write. Your hand was never as good as hers, nor as versatile. She could write the same poem in many different styles. You loved to watch her dip the brush in the ink and then with quick, sure flicks of her wrist, bring the paper to life. Her brush strokes were exquisitely precise, delicate as a night moth's wings, soft as a whisper. Her skill at calligraphy gave you an idea, a way to save her. You made her practice in her room, long after her lessons had ended.

Most women in China did not have these learning opportunities. Few Chinese women are remembered as poets or thinkers, the poetess Li Ch'ing Chao being a remarkable exception. Women, like eunuchs, were slaves, in a sense. This is another reason why it was considered an honor and a privilege to be a concubine, a sexual servant to the emperor. Yet a concubine has an unspoken duty to her master upon his death—if he requests her company in the hereafter. That is a polite way of saying the concubines would all be slain and buried with the dead emperor. I see you find that shocking. You are chilled by the very idea. So was Lotus. She possessed a rebellious spirit.

Lotus confided she did not want to go with the old man to his grave, even though all her sisters would be there too. They would all be buried alive together and go to Heaven as one family. When she told you that, you knew you must find a way to help her escape her destiny. Your fate was to be a eunuch—a eunuch enduring eternity in a watery hell until such time as a living person passed overhead, over the place where you drowned. But I'm getting ahead of myself. Be still, James. Take it like a man.

⊰⊱

The Dragon Boat festival, the last one you ever knew, was one of the best days of your life. You did not spend it with Lotus, however, but with your old friend Pau.

Having the day off, that fifth day of the fifth month of your fifteenth year, the two of you went to watch the boat races. You and Pau loved festival days, and the Dragon Boat festival was particularly exciting because of the races. And the water. What is it about water that is so alluring? A lake, a river, a canal, an ocean—water offers both pleasure and danger, both life and death. Water offers a means of escape and an unseen burial ground where our bodies are devoured by fishes and our spirits wait, unseen. Water connects us all and can consume us all.

Lotus was prohibited from going to the festival. She would have needed a sedan chair and two footmen to carry her, and there was no room on the crowded banks of the canal and along the narrow city streets, crowded on Dragon Boat Day, for sedan chairs. Although she longed to go along, you were secretly glad to have a day of freedom to enjoy the day with Pau. A raucous street festival is no place for an emperor's concubine, but it was certainly the place for two boys with a pocketful of silver taels to spend.

You lived your whole life in that one day, a windy blue day warmed by a smiling sun. No one else cared about two court eunuchs enjoying a day off, so we did as we pleased. Dressed in plain cotton trousers and yellow shirts, little blue caps covering your topknots, you might have been twins. You were practically invisible, for no one paid any attention to two young eunuchs wandering the streets, but you saw it all, heard it all, you drank it all in. Brightly painted dragon boats racing on the sparkling waters of the canal and high above, colorful kites tugged at their strings to be free. Music everywhere, lively tunes played by strolling musicians, and actors, dressed in fanciful costumes performed in the streets. Oh, the mouthwatering smells of food cooking! You bought moon cakes and dumplings, you stuffed your pockets with sweets to eat later. Pau won a pair of fine kid slippers in a betting game, and you squandered away more coins than you could afford, but it was the best day ever.

You had tea with Pau's friends, the sing-sing girls who lived on the pleasure boats docked along the canal. He brought them love poems from his masters, the scholars and administrators he worked for, and made arrangements with the old madam who kept the books for future romantic evenings afloat. Being a festival day, the girls had their leisure and had no clients to serve, and so they joined the two young eunuchs wandering the waterfront, clapping for the troupes of actors and puppeteers, and drinking far too much cheap rice wine.

I tell you this, James, so you can remember it in hell. Perhaps it will lessen your agony. At any rate, it lessens mine; it relieves me of a burden.

Lotus had asked you to bring her a bird, a song bird, one that could be trained to sit on her shoulder and sing. Everything could be bought at a festival. The bird vendors were there with their stacks of bamboo cages alongside the flower vendors, the fruit vendors, the lantern vendors. You chose a white nightingale in a wicker cage covered with a piece of white satin.

"But does it sing?" you demanded. "This bird is for the emperor's loveliest flower."

"If the bird is happy, she will sing," the old man said, scratching his long, wispy beard. "No one can make a bird sing if she's not happy."

You brought the bird in the cage back to the palace and presented it to Lotus. She was so very pleased she hugged you and planted kisses on your face with the glee of a child who has received a jujube. She named her bird Joy.

But the bird named Joy never sang. One day Lotus opened the cage, reached her slender hand in, and pulled the bird out in a flutter of wings, setting it gently on the window ledge.

"Fly away, you stupid bird. Go on. Leave me. I give you your freedom." When it did not fly she pushed it, angrily, as if she envied the freedom she was granting it. You both watched in horror as the bird tumbled two stories to the ground in a flutter of feathers and lay motionless. The bird's wings had been clipped so she could not escape. She could not fly.

"Like me. My feet were bound so that I could never escape my fate."

"Your feet are precious, as precious as your bud-like breasts. The emperor must love to hold them in his hands."

"I don't care. I wish I had big peasant feet. I wish I were ugly. I wish I were a eunuch. At least you have freedom." She looked at her dead bird, and her face contorted in grief, but she would not let me comfort her for some time. You wanted to tell her you weren't free, not at all. That you were as deformed as the bird whose wings had been clipped, and more deformed than she, with her tiny, useless, sensual feet.

You took the dead nightingale to the temple as a sacrifice. A few days later Lotus befriended a magpie, tempting it to her window ledge with bits of orange peel. The magpie couldn't sing, but it could talk; its voice was harsh but wise. Lotus fed her magpie all sorts of delicacies she took from her own plate.

"Eat," you urged. "You must keep up your strength, Lotus. You'll need it in the days to come."

"When I die, I want to be a magpie," she answered, and grew thinner by the day.

Chapter 3

"The emperor is dead!"

Those whispered words blew through the palace like a wildfire through dry autumn grasses.

Imagine it, James, if you can. Long before his death was officially announced, long before the gongs rang out with bone-jarring doom, long before the voices of a thousand grievers wailed in chorus, everyone inside the palace walls knew he was dead. But would his spirit return? Possibly. Emperor Zhu Yuanzhang (whose palace name was Taizu, and who called his reign Hongwu, which is what I shall call him) had been loath to leave the world he had ruled for these thirty years. It had taken him a long time to lose his grip on life. A three-day wait was decreed—to make certain his ghost would not change its mind and reclaim the body.

I don't want to hear any more of this story, I want to rejoin my own people. I try to recall their names, but Yu's voice fills my head, drowning out my own thoughts. I try to speak, but he puts his hand across my mouth. Gently.

Be still, James, and listen. About the emperor, you knew his time was coming. Everyone in the palace, from Hongwu's top advisors to the lowliest of servants, wondered what Hongwu's death would mean to them, personally. Some would gain favor with the new heir, Hongwu's studious young grandson. Others would be demoted, dismissed, exiled, or even executed. So it is, when one power replaces another. All those who are a threat are stamped out like embers.

A chosen few would accompany the emperor, called the Son of Heaven, to the next world—an honor of the highest sort. Already the concubines were ordering the most expensive silk fabric, jewelry, combs, and hairpins of the most exquisite material, as if they were preparing for an exotic journey. In a macabre sense, they were: it was a one-way journey to Heaven. Lotus, as one of the emperor's consorts, would be entombed with him. That was the custom. The expectation. The law.

I sense your abhorrence, James. But do not shut me out. You must know my history if you are to become me. I want you to know your life's story so you'll have something to ponder throughout your long nights in hell. But don't give up hope, for maybe someday after you have lived and relived your wretched existence again and again, you'll find someone to trade places with. No one wants to be Yu, the eunuch. The dead eunuch.

I feel his smile, his cold wet hand on my shoulder, gently, almost regretfully. I want to please him. If I please him, maybe he'll let me go?

Shall we continue? These things you must know. Hongwu was quite old when he died. He had accomplished many things during his reign. Born a peasant and brought up in a monastery, he was ambitious and tenacious as a shih tzu, becoming an expert in martial arts and warfare. He raised an army, and after more than thirty years of war, he succeeded in banishing the Mongol interlopers. It was Hongwu who reestablished Chinese rule and rebuilt the empire. He greatly enlarged Nanjing, adding to the ramparts that protected the city. It was the largest walled city in the world. He enlarged his family too, planted his seed and fathered twenty-six sons and sixteen daughters. At least, that was the official count. It was whispered in the palace and beyond that the women sapped his strength, little by little, stealing more of his yang. Yet in his prime, Hongwu had been one of China's greatest emperors.

His mind, they said, was slowly being taken over by devils and restless spirits. The great emperor began to mistrust everyone. Perhaps it was the result of the many concoctions of herbs and minerals the pharmacists were preparing in an effort to extend his life. Perhaps it was just because he was old.

For he was only a man—you were convinced of that, from the secrets Lotus shared with you. Not the Son of Heaven after all.

Lotus gave you all the intimate details of his body, describing even his private parts, shriveled and limp, unresponsive to the artful strokes she applied with her agile little hands.

"Just lie beside me, my sweet little bird," he wheezed, his breath smelling of decay. "Lie here and sing me a dream. I want to go to Heaven in your arms."

One by one the emperor's bodily functions shut down. The servants who emptied his chamber pot whispered that the great Son of Heaven's bowel movements had become a fetid black river. His royal urine became a dark amber color, thick as syrup. Then brown, dwindling to a trickle, and then ceasing altogether. His face and hands and feet had puffed up and his mind joined the ghosts of his ancestors many days before his heart admitted defeat.

Hongwu's reign had lasted many decades, and although he ruled with a harsh hand, he had put the Chinese back in control and brought prosperity. Or maybe the industrious people had made their own good fortune. In any case, the emperor was dead.

The palace began to prepare for his real funeral procession—and the decoy procession staged to fool the grave robbers as well as the emperor's brothers who were already planning to take power. In your new world, James, you'll discover that deception is so important; it's the key to everything.

Hongwu had planned his own funeral, it was to be the grandest, most elaborate the world had ever known. His tomb was a fortress, it had taken many years to build. The old warrior emperor left sealed instructions explaining how he was to be immortalized. He would be accompanied to the next world by his favorite horses, his pall bearers, and forty-two of his concubines. All would be sealed in the tomb with him. If at the last minute they panicked, their throats would be cut. Hongwu would rule in the underworld as he had ruled in this life.

This is what concerned me, James. This you need to know. This is what had been occupying your mind and heart for weeks—ever since Lotus had whispered her secret in your eager ear. It was considered the highest honor a woman could have: to be chosen as one of the emperor's concubines, and then to accompany him to the next world, upon his death. But Lotus wanted to live in this world, whatever the cost. She asked you to help her escape her fate, her pleading eyes, her grip on your arm making you feel like the man you could never be as a eunuch. It was a shocking request, to go against Imperial orders, to go against tradition. To go against destiny itself, refusing the great honor the emperor had bestowed upon her—to serve him in Heaven's bed until the end of time.

Lotus shocked you with her confession, yet you were only too eager to do her bidding. You would gladly risk your own flesh to save hers. A plan you had to devise, or it would all end badly, and she would be executed and go to Hell instead of Heaven with the emperor. Likely you would both end up in hell anyway—but at least there would be the chance for life first. And what is life but a painful procession of pain and uncertainties? Yet we crave it, don't we? The fear, the hope, the pleasure, the pain. Don't struggle so, James. It is your fate to trade places with me.

When I am you, James, I will live your life like you never have dared. You have had every opportunity, yet you waste your life, you fritter it away. It has made me angry to watch you throw it away. I will live your life as it deserves to be lived. I will be your best self, James, while you take my place in hell and learn what desire means. The same with your friends. And no one will be the wiser. No one will even realize you are gone. We are a harsh people, my friend. The Buddha brought us peace and equanimity but not love. The goddess Quan Yin, she has compassion for us. All-encompassing, unconditional love, a most rare thing in our society. What she has to offer is better than a mother's love, better than sexual pleasures. In times of sorrow, Quan Yin understands. She comforts us, never scolds. You will be crying out for Quan Yin when you become me. Here, I give you this likeness of her to wear around your neck on the bottom of the ocean, so you don't forget. Now she is ever near your heart. When your spirit calls out to her, she will hear and she will be near. She cannot save you, but she forgives, she understands, she loves the most wretched of us.

Yu is crying. His stifled sobs sound like my own. Maybe they are.

Chapter 4

The emperor had not summoned any of his concubines for seven days, not even to lie beside him to purr like kittens for his comfort. It was whispered the great ruler was already halfway into the next world; his mind and spirit were already in Heaven, only his body remained behind. Any day now, any hour, the dreaded death gong would sound, and Lotus, along with her sister concubines, would be taken to the tomb with the Emperor Hongwu.

The emperor had forbidden his sons to attend his funeral. They were to remain in their principalities, for Hongwu knew they would want to seize control from his designated heir, Prince Jianwen. Hongwu decreed his sons must be contained—imprisoned, if necessary—to prevent them from seizing power.

Prince Jianwen was a young man of twenty-two. He was already married, as was the custom, with a son of his own. Jianwen also had two concubines, purchased for him by his grandfather when he was just coming of age, also the custom. They kept him amused and instructed him in the ways of love until a suitable, high-born girl worthy of being empress could be found. It mattered not if they were attracted to one another; marriages were too important to be left to the whim of young love.

The prince was a very serious and devout man. He did not care for power, he sought truth. You often saw him at the temple studying with the monks or sitting on a garden bench lost in a book. You liked him; he had a poet's heart. He wanted to change the world through ideas. If Lotus had to belong to an emperor, to share his bed on demand, why not Jianwen?

⊰⊱

With expert hands the servant unpinned Lotus's hair, coiled elaborately on top of her head. Strand by strand, her tresses fell onto her shoulders. The servant massaged Lotus's scalp and combed her hair, rubbing sweet-smelling oil into it. The scent filled the air and pierced your heart with longing for what you could not experience. It was a concoction of oils made especially for Lotus; it was her own personal perfume. You stood by the door breathing in her perfume and watching the flicker of candlelight throw shadows onto the ceiling. Outside, the voices of the insects, the steady chirping of crickets, set you on edge. They seemed to be warning *get out, get out, get out while you can!*

As soon as the servant had been dismissed, Lotus sprang out of bed. "More light, Yu. We need more lanterns." She rummaged to the bottom of her lacquered chest where she kept the scrolls, the ink, and the brushes. You returned with two lanterns blazing, and she was ready to work. Her black eyes shone with anticipation—and with fear. If your plan worked, she would not accompany the old emperor to the next world but would have a chance to live longer in this world. She would be presented to the new emperor as a gift from his departed grandfather, the great Hongwu. The gift of the virgin Lotus.

You whispered in her lovely ear the words, and she turned them into characters on the paper. She wrote in a bold flourish, mimicking the emperor's own hand. The words were your only hope, and that hope came alive on the rice paper scroll.

"A living gift of the lotus blossom, most pure." You spoke softly, lest anyone should hear.

"To my grandson, my heir, whose reign shall be called Jianwen—establishing civility—I have saved this flower, untouched, for you. May she be a companion, may she serve you with joy, and may she produce many sons, all strong, wise and good. May our dynasty last for ten thousand years."

"Now sign his name," you whispered, kissing the delicate curled rim of her ear. She paused, clutching the pendant that hung between her peony bud breasts, and invoked Quan Yin, the goddess of compassion. Then she dipped her brush and began making the symbols that were the emperor's name. As soon as the ink had dried you rolled them up and took the scrolls to Pau so that he could make them legitimate with the emperor's own seal.

You were all guilty of crimes punishable by death. Pau, why did he risk his life? He did it for you because he was your friend.

James, you and I are trading places in this dream. Bit by bit, memory by memory, can you feel it? I becoming James; James becoming Yu. Right now we are all mixed up together, but soon the exchange will be complete. Let me finish telling the story so that you know the rest of Yu's short, tragic life. The full moon approaches its zenith and the ship is passing over the place where you drowned over seven hundred years ago.

No! Get off me, get out of my head!

Shh. Be still. Be a good lad. Don't make me use force.

Yu's laugh, high pitched like a girl's.

Listen. Let me tell you the tragic end of the story. Your story. Where were we? Ah, yes. You made your escape the night the emperor was drawing his last, labored breaths. Everyone was preoccupied and paid you no mind. You slipped out dressed as a lowly servant emptying human waste carried in large tightly woven baskets. A night soil man. The guards held their breath and averted their eyes as you passed through the south gate with a pole over your shoulders, one basket suspended from each end. Indeed, one basket was filled with imperial shit. The other one held Lotus, crouching, hugging her knees to her chest.

The magpie followed you, flitting from tree to tree. And then you followed the magpie down to the canal where you blended in with the laborers, the gamblers, the transients.

That night the emperor died, passing quietly in his sleep. The concubine in his bed was immediately killed, her throat slit right there in the bed. Three days later, Emperor Hongwu's death was officially announced, the gongs struck, and the wailers summoned. You and Lotus were far away by then. Thirty miles down the river on a pleasure boat, biding your time. Pau had arranged it with the sing-sing girls.

The very day Emperor Hongwu was laid to rest in the great mausoleum, forty-two of his women were entombed with him, buried alive so as to keep their beauty intact for the next world. They were left to suffocate together, sisters in death. Some of them had to be drugged and some of them had to have their hands and feet bound, but most went willingly, if terrified. They were proud to do their duty. Ah, such a waste, such a waste of human life. But in the Middle Kingdom human lives were cheap. You'll see. As cheap as grains of rice.

At least Lotus was not among them. Yu had seen to that. Yu—You!—had helped her escape death, but now what? The two of you were accustomed to luxury, living in the emperor's palace with servants to attend you. Now you were paying guests on a pleasure boat with the sing-sing girls. When the new emperor proclaimed the mourning was over, you came back upriver, back to the palace and presented Lotus, along with the letter written on imperial paper by what appeared to be the dead emperor's own hand and secured with his seal. You made quite a stir, carrying Lotus wrapped up in an exquisite piece of silk to be unwrapped only by Jianwen.

And so Lotus became the young emperor's consort. You carried her to his bedchamber that night and waited outside until morning to carry her back to her own room. Pau came to wait with you, to keep you company, to rejoice in the success of the plan. And though you tried, you ached inside, knowing what was going on behind those doors. Yet this was the best possible scenario. This was as good as it gets for a young eunuch.

Lotus was strangely content. She now had a purpose in life: she would bear the emperor a child, hopefully a male child, which our world values more. It hurt you to see her so happy, even though her happiness is what you wanted most. How can that be? The pain filled your chest, making it difficult to breathe. You could never be what you wanted to be—you had to settle for protecting her, being her companion, her friend. Night after night, you carried Lotus to Jianwen's room, wrapped up in silk, her tiny feet never touching the floor. Your bird with clipped wings, you loved her so. Lotus grew to love the new emperor and the emperor loved her. How could he not? It broke your heart, but you were still alive. With life, all things are possible.

Chapter 5

The young emperor had enemies. The princes, his jealous uncles, all wanted to seize the throne. Each saw himself as the rightful heir to a kingdom; none were content with a mere principality. Old Hongwu had seen to the physical separation of his many sons, giving them lands far from the capital city of Nanjing in order to keep the peace. To further protect his precious grandson and chosen heir, Hongwu had decreed that the other princes should not attend his funeral.

But that only delayed trouble. The princes formed their alliances, raised their armies, and began marching toward Nanjing. A takeover was only a matter of time. Being prince just would not do, especially when you are subservient to your nephew, a studious, soft-hearted boy raised by women, scholars, and monks, his head filled with poetry and the teachings of the Buddha. A boy with no experience in martial arts, a boy who had never commanded an army. That was our Jianwen, the compassionate emperor we so gladly served. Jianwen, the emperor we would die for.

Young Jianwen's closest advisors tried to forestall the inevitable. They managed to derail several coups and had five uncles imprisoned. Two more uncles died of supposedly natural causes, though you wondered if maybe they were murdered. But one uncle no one could stop was Zhu Di, the Prince of Yan. This power hungry man had rallied his troops. He was coming down from Beijing armed and dangerous, intending to kill his young nephew and take over the palace. Lotus would be ravaged; you and Pau would die by the sword.

⊰⊱

Relive with me these last days of your pitiful life. There was widespread panic as Zhu Di's army marched closer, closer. The hooves of a thousand horses raised a cloud of red dust that could be seen on the horizon. In the city the people prepared for the invasion. Many ran to the hills, taking their families and their household goods with them.

In the palace the emperor made haste to flee for his life. His advisors had failed him, there was nothing to do but stay and fight or go into hiding. Jianwen was not a fighting man, and besides, it would have been suicide to fight his uncle and his strong army. The young emperor's guards had deserted him, his own small force was falling apart. He sent the empress and her baby into hiding at a monastery in the mountains. He would join them later.

You had devised a plan to save Lotus's life, Pau's life, and your own. You were willing to fight, to die—but you didn't want to die in vain. You had risked so much for Lotus, and now she was carrying another life inside—she was pregnant with Jianwen's own child.

You dared to approach the young emperor with your rash plan, you had nothing to lose. You would have done it anyway, but you wanted his approval. His blessing. Jainwen gave you permission, he was desperate.

"Just so no innocents are sacrificed," he said. The young emperor was indeed a soft-hearted man, for your kingdom was built on the blood of innocents. But Jianwen wanted a peaceable world. He wanted an end to ignorance and poverty, an end to senseless killing and corruption. He wanted a kingdom ruled justly. He studied the teachings of Confucius and practiced the way of the Buddha; he prayed to the goddess of compassion, Quan Yin, for assistance. Jianwen was too good for this wicked world.

⊰⊱

That afternoon Leili, one of Lotus's servants, a toothless old woman, bent and dry as a twig, dropped dead while sweeping the floor. Lotus was in a music class at the time, and you had gone back to her chamber to fetch a robe, for the air had turned cold. Razor sharp. A storm was moving in.

Seeing the old woman dead on the floor, still holding the broomstick, you felt no sadness at all for the servant whose spirit had decamped to a better world, surely. Instead, a star of opportunity shone over her. What serendipity! It was as if she had laid down her humble existence for you and for Lotus. Your heart leaped inside your ribcage as you pulled Leili's body into the closet and covered her with a blanket.

When you brought Lotus back to her room after her lessons had ended for the day, you whispered your plan. There was little time, for rumors were flying that Prince Zhu Di and his army were growing closer and gaining strength. But for your scheme to work, you needed more dead bodies.

You told Pau of your plan, and he was eager to assist. That evening you left the palace and went beyond the city walls to the road leading north, the same road the army was following on its march south. Here, you waited for a corpse walker to come along. The corpse walkers frequented this road, for many peasants had left the countryside seeking a better life in the Imperial City, but they all wanted to be buried in their homeland alongside their ancestors. For this assurance of eternal peace, they would pay a corpse walker, or their family paid for one, to bring the dead body home. This often took many days or even weeks. Meanwhile, the corpse began to bloat and rot, unless it had been embalmed, a process that was beyond the means of many. Then too, a corpse walker often had to deal with angry spirits. It was a most unlucky occupation, and only the most desperate men resorted to it.

You paid the first corpse walker you saw for the body he had been entrusted to carry. You paid him in silver, more money than he ever had in his life, and he asked you no questions. Bowing, he slipped away, hoping the dead man's spirit wouldn't notice he had abandoned it—or worse—sold it for money. But you didn't care about angry ghosts, you needed a body. Any body. You already had dead people angry at you, so one more wouldn't matter. There was Lotus's servant whose corpse was hidden in the closet. And there was the dead emperor himself, who by now must realize he had been tricked out of his youngest concubine, the virgin with the tiniest feet. But, the peasant's spirit should be grateful. The body would be cremated, an honor reserved for monks. Its funeral pyre would be inside the Imperial Palace within the Son of Heaven's own chambers.

The corpse was wrapped in a shroud, and the strong smell of spices masked any odor of decay. The rigor mortis had passed, and the body was no longer stiff, but limp as a sea cucumber—almost too willing to go along with you. You were afraid an arm might fall off as you tried to get a grip on it. Believe me, you were glad for the tightly wound cloth that held everything in place and hid the face. Especially the eyes. It was well known that if the corpse's eyes were covered, the spirit couldn't see what was going on around it.

I can see you are appalled, but trust me: depravity soon becomes routine. The more an evil act is repeated, the easier it becomes to do. And soon it no longer becomes repulsive. It seems commonplace. The human soul shrivels and becomes so small and dry it can easily blow away in the wind or be crushed by a heavy heel. Yet you did what you had to do to save Lotus's life. You did it for love.

❦

Slowly you made your way along the road, singing softly to the dead body to soothe it. To trick it. Travelers stepped aside, giving you a wide berth, for they could see you were walking a corpse home. They covered their eyes; they held their breath; they did not speak. For there is no gain to be had in looking at a corpse, there is no reason to acknowledge it unless you have something to offer for its journey or its afterlife.

As you shuffled along the path through the darkness, you could see the glow from the campfires of Prince Zhu Di's army camped outside the city walls. You had gotten the second body just in time. Even if your plan worked, you might still be killed—but you would be a hero. If it didn't work, you would just be killed. Either way, you'd be dead sooner or later. You were already going to some form of hell, so what did it matter? You wanted to make the most of the remaining days of this brief earthly existence, all the more valuable for its transient shimmer. Transient and spectacular as a spark that bursts into flame but soon disappears.

Back at the palace, chaos ruled. Many of the emperor's advisors and department heads had already packed their belongings and fled. Servants were looting what was left behind as they prepared to run. Any hour now and the palace walls would be breached—the guards had already deserted their posts.

No one paid any attention to a corpse walker that night, dragging a body. Pau and Lotus helped you drag both corpses into the emperor's bedroom. You stripped them of their rags and dressed them in red imperial silks, the emperor's and empress's own clothes. You placed them in an embrace and then spilled lantern oil over them and around the room. With a torch, you ignited the oil and watched in awe as the flames leaped up and devoured the room, consuming everything but the stone walls themselves.

Meanwhile, Emperor Jianwen and his remaining family dressed themselves in peasant clothes and slipped away through the secret underground passageway. You and Pau, carrying Lotus between you, followed them as the fire spread through the palace, fanned by the autumn wind blowing down from the mountains. Do you feel breathless? You were breathless that night; your chest felt as if it were about to burst.

You ran through the night, following the canal to where a certain pleasure boat waited and the sing-sing girls welcomed you aboard. The boatman and his crew took you to the river and from there to the sea where Jianwen purchased a sea-going junk and a crew of pirates to sail her. Word had reached the harbor that the palace had gone up in a series of explosions, thanks to the trail of gunpowder you and Pau had laid.

Hours later, after the flames had burned themselves out, the charred remains of the emperor and empress were discovered inside the royal chamber. Your ruse had worked—for the time being.

Jianwen, with his consorts and few loyal attendants, planned to sail to a distant port and seek safe haven in a monastery. Lotus was a few weeks pregnant, she was feeling tired and nauseated. You spoon-fed her rice water from a wooden ladle to keep her strength up. Her smile was your reward. There could be no other reward, not for you.

After a few weeks at sea, the sickness passed. Lotus began to eat and the color crept back into her cheeks. You washed her hair in a pail of rainwater. You rubbed her skin with scented oil, cradling her lotus buds in your hands.

Pau had learned to navigate from the pirates, who found his uncanny memory to be very useful. That gift of his, the way he could look at something and understand it. The understanding it takes most men a lifetime to learn, Pau absorbed as if by magic. He could be a great help to the emperor, who recognized his talents and promised him a position in the new order.

But Pau didn't care about his standing; he didn't care about money or influence. He only wanted to play with his quicksilver knowledge to amuse himself the way a child plays with blocks. Jianwen, our young emperor-in-hiding, would have made such a difference. He had the beginnings of wisdom, a curious mind, and a compassionate heart. Jianwen would have led the people into a new era of civility.

⊰⊱

Zheng He, eunuch admiral of the Ming fleet, was incredibly lucky; fate was on his side. Or perhaps the pirates played you wrong? You'll never know. So many truths are buried alive and forgotten. But one night you saw his ships on the horizon. The magnificent spread of sails, the wings of a fleet of warships, ghostly in the moonlight. They were hunting you down, they were hell bent to destroy Jianwen and his family.

You didn't fool them, not for long. They weren't convinced the charred bodies they found in the palace were the emperor and empress. Zhu Di had sent them out to search for us—and to destroy any vessel harboring the exiled nephew and his family. Their junks were bigger and faster than yours, they bore down on you like *mong chin*, those fierce birds of prey diving for the kill.

You scrambled for the crossbows and arrows, Pau for the catapult to launch bombs and fireballs. You stoked up the braziers, you sharpened your swords. Jianwen, who was not a fighter, not trained in martial arts but in the peaceful philosophy of the Buddha, stood by you, halberd in hand, ready to defend himself and his family to the death.

Below, the women hid with their short *daos,* their butterfly swords, concealed under the folds of their silk robes. They would defend themselves, they would plunge those knifes into their attacker's guts, their throats. They would not be taken without a fight. All they ever wanted in this life was to live and to bring forth life. They would die trying to defend this right.

When the lead ship came within range, Pau launched an iron ball wrapped in burning rags. Though you were doomed, you cheered as the sail caught fire, fanned by the air moving across it. Pau launched another fireball, and you cheered as it found its mark. You readied your crossbow, the arrows resting in the bucket of coals. As soon as the attacking ship was close enough, you fired an arrow onto the deck and then reached for another.

But on they came, the lead ship was about to smash into yours. Warriors jumped aboard from the blunt bow of their warship. Like so many rats they poured aboard, brandishing their *chang daos,* their long swords, screaming, "Death to the traitors! Bloody red death!" Remember well the rage you felt in those last minutes, the rage that filled you as the heat seared your body and the sword's edge found its mark. Remember Lotus, down below with the women, fighting for her life. The last thing you heard was her scream.

No! I want to live!

So do I, James. But only one of us can have this body.

Chapter 19

"James!" Ming's voice comes from the surface. I'm floating up toward it. "James, are you alive?" Ming's hands are touching my hand, my cheek. The smell of burning kerosene and the yellow glow of lantern light. Yu's grip on me dissolves, the weight of his soul is lifted from my chest. It's the flame and Ming's own aura, a light as warm and pulsating as the lantern's glow that sends him fleeing to darkness. I feel Ming's hands, those tiny, capable hands, under my shoulders. She's dragging me free, she's helping me to sit up, she holds my face in her hands.

"What are you doing down here? I couldn't find you, I was worried sick!" She pulls me to my feet, she's yanking my arm. "Come on! There's a ship passing on the horizon. This is our chance to be rescued!"

I'm caught between two worlds, my head feels foggy. Is this really Ming or is it Lotus? They look alike except for the feet. Looking down, I see she's wearing sport sandals with round rubber toe guards, like bumpers. Big feet, a warrior's shoes, not a concubine's crippled feet. And she's wearing the jade pendant. I see a piece of my face in the mirror on her chest. James's face, not Yu's.

"James!" She pulls my hand and I'm following. "Let's go! We can't let them pass without seeing us." Ming scrambles up the ladder and I'm close on her heels. I slam the hatch, the gateway to hell. I lock it down, as if that could stop them—the dead who want to live again.

On deck, the air is fresh and salty clean. I drink it in, filling my lungs and washing my mind. A breeze cools my cheek and ruffles my hair, at last the wind has come back. Overhead, the moon looks down with its big white face and its crooked smile. The sky's all milky, the sea is liquid silver. Is this the dream, or is Yu's world the dream? The throbbing pain in my head tells me I'm awake now. Wide awake.

"Look there! See the lights?" She's gripping my arm so hard it hurts. "No, over there, James!" I look where her finger's pointing, I try to concentrate on what she's saying. My throat burns for lack of water.

It's a ship, yes. But can I trust my eyes? The voices are silent. I have no premonition, no knowledge. Still, my chest fills with hope, it feels like a song.

"We have to attract their attention," Ming says. "Lights—we need more lights. We need to run a lantern up the mast. Help me, James."

"Where's everybody else? Where's Bastien?"

"They're all below. Passed out. Drunk. Except Truman, he's on the foredeck. He's built a catapult. He's going to light the emergency flares and launch them. There's no talking to him right now, he's obsessed with the damned thing. But I don't want to rely on the catapult, we have to send a light up the mast right now, so the ship can see us. You have to pull yourself together, James. I need you!"

I help her gather up more lanterns from the saloon. We fill them with kerosene and light them, turning the wicks up high so they'll burn really bright. With pieces of rope we used for knot practice, we tie the rings on top of the lanterns to the main halyard. We haul them up to the masthead, high above the deck.

"Now lower it a few feet and raise it again. Like a signal. To get their attention," Ming instructs.

"If they saw us, wouldn't they answer back?"

"They're probably calling us right now on the radio. We've got to let them know we need help!"

Truman calls to us, he's ready to light the first flare and launch it into the sky. But the first one's a dud, it sputters and goes out. So is the next one. And the next. They're all duds, they're probably expired. Too old and not operable, like everything else aboard this boat. And the ship on the horizon has already moved further away. If we don't hurry and get their attention, they'll soon be out of sight.

"We need more light," Ming says. "Torches! Let's make some torches. We can use the spare battens, the bamboo poles that stiffen the sails. We can tie dish towels or tee shirts around the tops and dip them in kerosene. Light them on fire and wave them around so the other ship sees us."

"You do that," says Truman. "I'm going to make a bomb for my catapult."

Ming and I make torches. We line them up on the deck, tie them to the rail with a running half hitch. But Truman's right—we need to get the light higher into the air. Our lanterns at the masthead give off a weak, flickering light. We need something bright and spectacular.

Truman's collected the rest of the cabbages from the galley. They're all black and rotting. With a rigging knife and a spoon he hollows one out and shoves a roll of toilet paper inside. Puts the cabbage in the catapult basket, drenches the toilet paper roll with kerosene, and lights it. It burns like a trash can fire.

"Now watch this! Stand back, you guys. Hold your ears! Fire in the hole!" He trips the rope. The counterweight, an old cannonball suspended by a piece of cargo netting, drops down, and the catapult arm swings over, hurling the flaming rotten vegetable up and out over the ocean. Red embers trail it, like a comet's tail.

"Awesome!" Truman screams. "Let's make some more!" He's in his glory. He would go down happy, as long as he was shooting something.

❆

The ship's lights are brighter, we can see a red port light and a green starboard light. It's heading our way! I scramble to the main halyard to lower and raise the lanterns—a signal, a salute. Ming's calling to the others to wake up and come on deck, we're about to be rescued. She grabs me and hugs me, she's so relieved, and I hug her back. We dance around in a circle, hopping up and down, while Truman fires off the last cabbage and toilet paper bomb.

Now Ming breaks away and runs to the rail, grabs a torch, and starts waving it. I follow her, but something's wrong. The hairs stand up on my arms and on the back of my neck, it's not the breeze I'm feeling. Something's about to happen, something awful—I don't know what. I watch in horror as the water parts, like when Moses was being chased and the waters parted for him to cross. Look! A huge crack, a hole in the middle of the ocean—a bottomless pit—like the black hole in my mind. We're going to be drawn into it, we're sliding to the edge. But then we stop, and I'm looking down into black space.

Out of the dark depths they rise, lit by the white light of the moon, a terrifying sight. Huge ships, a whole fleet of four-masted junks, ancient Chinese warships armed with catapults and soldiers, trained to kill. Their tattered sails are filled with an unholy wind, their pennants fly again from the mastheads. The fierce, painted eyes on the ships' hulls have spied us through time and space. They're bearing down on us, these ghost ships. It's Zhu Di's imperial fleet, they've come up out of the deep and out of the past, but this is no residual haunting. These demons, these *shui gui*, want our lives. We've crossed the place where they went down over seven hundred years ago. Tonight, the full moon of the Hungry Ghost Month, they've been released from hell.

The closest ship fires a bomb that hits our foredeck and bursts into flames. We all cower in fear. A storm of burning arrows rains down on us. Here they come, they're almost close enough to leap on board. I can see them, silk robes blowing in the wind, their long swords gleaming.

Now Bastien, Colton, and Myer come running up on deck to join us. They have guns, they've got Mr. Miles and Captain Dan's pistols. They're shooting at the invaders. But there are so many, too many, and they're not falling—they keep coming. You can't kill a ghost with a bullet, they're already dead.

"James! Take the helm and steer us away!" It's Ming. She's setting the mizzen sail, and I stumble across the deck and take hold of the tiller. "Let's outrun them!" She hurries to the mainmast, brings down the lanterns, and hauls up the mainsail. It snaps and cracks as it fills with air. *Good Fortune* has sprouted her wings, we're flying on the wind. But the sails have caught fire, the foredeck is burning where the bomb struck. Smoke! Now smoke's coming up out of the companionway. Fire, belowdecks!

Up the ladder staggers Steff, bandanna over her nose, broken Hana Bay rum bottle in her hand. She's holding it by the neck, she's ready to defend herself. It'll cut a human to ribbons, but ghosts don't bleed. Fire slows them down—but fire can destroy us as well. Only our combined life force can stop them, I know that now. If we're alone, they can kill us, they can take our bodies for their own. But if we're all together, if we join hands like we did that day on deck when we dropped Captain Dan over the side, if we laughed together or cried together, they wouldn't have a chance. They want what we have.

But where's Yu in all of this? Why isn't he here to fight for my life? He wanted it more than anything.

A blinding white flash, the ship rocks, I'm jerked into the air like a sock puppet and thrown to the deck. My mouth fills with warm blood. The noise of the explosion splits my eardrums and rings in my bones. I look up, see Truman, his face black, his hair on fire. He's screaming, but I can't hear his voice. I see his open mouth. He's beating his head with his hands, he starts to run toward the rail.

"Truman! No! Stop!" I'm dragging myself across the deck. I'm grabbing his ankles. I'm pulling him down. He falls and I crawl on top of him to smother the flames. Like I should have done for my father, the night our house burned down.

Truman and I struggle to our feet. Embers rain down, we're stamping them out but not fast enough. Like a bad dream, we're moving too slowly. It's like running through wet cement. Just like in my nightmares, I will myself to rise up and fly away, out of their reach. But I can't. I'm powerless. This is my premonition coming true.

"Here they come," Truman yells. "They're coming aboard!"

The dead ones cross the transom, seaweed clinging to their dripping robes, their skulls covered with barnacles. They've come to take our ship, to take our souls. A figure looms over me, a cloaked warrior with a burned-out face, gaping holes where his eyes once were. He's holding a long, curved sword above his head. He lunges, swinging, but I duck. The sword swishes past, striking the deck. I grab a burning torch and stick it right through him. He's not solid, not flesh and blood, but he's real, all right. Real as a bolt of lightning. His force feels like a kick in the chest, hurling me backward. I'm on the deck, the breath knocked out of me, and the torch has rolled out of my reach. It catches a coil of rope on fire. I hear the others shouting. I hear Ming calling out to me, she's calling my name.

It's too late to save our *Good Fortune*, there's fire down below. We should abandon ship, but we don't have a lifeboat—the dinghy is gone. Mr. Miles took it and never returned. Ming's over by the locker with the red cross on it, the one labeled LIFE JACKETS. She's pulling out the orange vests, she's handing them out. She's putting one on, just like we practiced. She looks as calm as a flight attendant giving a safety demonstration.

The masts are starting to burn. Bastien grabs the axe out of the locker. He runs to the main mast, hacking at the intruders on his way. He's swinging like a mad man. What the hell is he doing?

"Let go the sheets!" he yells. The sound of the axe rings out. Bastien's hacking at the mast like a lumberjack chopping down a tree. A Chinese warrior comes up behind him. He's got a spear. He raises it over his shoulder, but Colton and Myer jump him together. They go crashing to the deck, and the ghost vanishes in a puff of smoke. Bastien is still swinging the axe, he's almost through. With a groan the mast falls, taking a chunk of the rail with it. Into the water it drops, the flaming sail hissing and steaming. Bastien has made us a life raft.

"She's going to blow!" he shouts. "Get off! Get off the boat! The propane tank, it's going to explode any minute!"

The others are strapped into their life jackets and follow Ming over the side. Even Truman, whose catapult is in flames. He swims for the mast. The fan-shaped mainsail, stiffened with bamboo battens, floats next to it, providing a platform.

"What are you waiting for?" Bastien shouts at me. "Save yourself!"

Setting the course so *Good Fortune* is headed away from the raft, I tie the tiller to the rail. My last act as helmsman. The ship falls off and begins to sail away, the wind fanning the flaming mizzen and foresail. I'm hurrying to put on my life vest, but what is Bastien doing? He's going below. Why is he going below? It's on fire. The propane tank for the stove is going to explode. He's probably going for Steff, he doesn't know she's already on the raft. He thinks she's still passed out in his bed, he's going to rescue her.

The others are calling to us, they're clinging to the mast, which is already behind us. *Good Fortune* is a fire ship now. A junk can't be sunk, but it can burn up. It can explode. We have but one chance to live.

"Bastien!" I scream as loud as I can, my throat raw. He doesn't hear me. I run to the companionway, step down onto the ladder's first rung. But I can't go down any further, the heat and the smoke are unbearable.

"Bastien!" I call again. "Steff is safe, she's with us!" The smoke fills my chest, I'm choking. I can't breathe! I can't go down any further. "Dad! Dad, wake up!" The smoke is making me cry. I have to save myself, it's all I can do. I'm sorry, Dad. I can't help you. Forgive me!

Grabbing the oars that Mr. Miles left behind, I'm climbing over the rail. My knees are shaking. Suck in a big breath and with a leap of faith, launch off into space.

Freefalling…For an instant, time stands still.

I hit the water hard, the ocean swallows me. Something grabs my ankles, pulls me down, but the life vest pops me to the surface. The oars, where are the oars? There's one, I manage to reach it. I hold it out in front of me, kicking and thrashing, making my way to the floating mast, the mast that Bastien cut down to save us.

The sail is awash with water, but it's still attached to the mast. The bamboo battens keep it from sinking. The pennant at the masthead ripples under the water like an eel. The others are huddled together, whimpering and crying. I toss the oar up onto the sail and then grab hold of the log. With my remaining strength, I heave myself up.

We've tied ourselves to the mast with the halyard and the sheets to keep the waves from washing us off. We're shivering, we're thirsty, we're exhausted. We're alive.

But who am I? Am I James or am I Yu? It's James's body, I'm pretty sure, though I don't want to let go of the mast to feel between my legs to make sure. I'm wearing James's clothes. But who am I inside?

"Yu!"

There's no answer.

"Dad!"

If he hears me, he doesn't answer back.

In my mind's eye, I can see a ship coming toward us. Someone on watch saw the fireballs we launched, someone saw the burning sails, the ghost fleet who attacked us. All aboard must've heard the explosion, and now they're headed this way to pick up the survivors. It's the law of the sea. They'll see us in the moonlight. They've got many hands and cargo nets to haul us aboard. They've got water and food for us, they'll take us to land. To China or Japan, I don't care. Dry land is all that matters. What kind of ship—a container ship, a coast-guard cutter, a sailing vessel, Noah's Ark—I have no idea. What language they speak, I don't have a clue. I don't even know what time we're in. Mine or Yu's?

Next to me Ming is huddled on the canvas raft. She's curled like a sea horse, her wet hair shines. She gives off a weak aura of crystalized light, like a halo around the moon. The pendant, she's still wearing the pendant around her neck. The pendant will guide the ship to us. Mazu is with us, she's been protecting us all along. Who is the other goddess, the one with the kind face? What's her name? The one on the cover of the book? Quan Yin, that's it. Quan Yin, the goddess of compassion, she's our kind and loving grandmother. She hugs my neck. Quan Yin and Jesus. I think of him too. A picture comes to mind, a picture in Gran's bible. A painting of Jesus in a white robe. He's got a kind, sad face. A golden light comes out of his head. He's walking on water, on the Sea of Galilee, his thin arm outstretched. He's saving some fishermen, their boat capsized in a storm. Maybe he can save us. Mazu will guide him to us. She's the man on watch who points to something on the water, alerting the officer on the deck to change course. I call out to all three of them—to anybody who might hear me.

"Help us!" That's my prayer. My voice is barely a squeak, but it's out there now. My words, rising, escaping the atmosphere, gathering speed, bouncing around the universe, ricocheting off of all the other words that have ever been spoken, a holy cacophony out there in space.

I don't hear anything but the roar of the ocean in my ears. It's like background noise, the drone of a fan. I'm so tired. I want to drift off to sleep, to take a little nap until we're rescued. The voices in my head are sleeping, it's kind of peaceful. Except I'm cold.

Help us. My words come back to me like an echo. I move closer to Ming, who's huddled against Truman, who's curled against Steff, who's holding onto Colton, who's holding onto Myer. There's safety and warmth in numbers. But we're missing one.

Chapter 20

The sharks are moving toward us, a dark mass of churning water. I see glimpses of their dorsal fins breaking the water. The oar, where's the oar? I can hit them with it, I can defend us. But I can't find the oar. It's gone. It must've washed away.

"Ming?" She seems to be sleeping. Her right arm is draped across the mast, alongside mine, her lips are blue in the moonlight. Her skin feels cold and smooth as sea glass. She could be dead. But when I put my face next to hers, I feel her warm breath on my cheek. I press my shivering lips to hers and taste salt. Her eyes open. She blinks and looks at me with the trace of a smile on her face.

"I was having the nicest dream." She closes her eyes and another wave washes over us. I wrap my arms around her slim shoulders, and pull her close to me. She slips her arms around my waist, under my life vest, and warms her hands against my back.

The sharks are circling us, they're closing in. They're ravenous, they're thirsty for our blood. I hear them thrashing in the water. I have to fight them off. Pulling away from Ming's body, I raise my arm to strike out—but wait—those aren't sharks. They're dolphins! I see their sleek backs breaking the water as they swim up and down, up and down. So many of them, must be hundreds, and they're leaping and diving, half flying, half swimming. I smell their warm breath, I hear them blowing as they come up for air. In the moonlight, I see the gleaming of their tiny teeth.

And now I see something else—a bobbing head and thrashing arms. Not dolphin, a human form, but who is it? One of the ghost warriors? Yu? Bastien? I don't see the bright orange of a life jacket, and the head is low in the water. He's swimming through hills and valleys of water. He's swimming with the dolphins, the dolphins are bringing him to our life raft. But he's struggling, he's disoriented. He turns to look back at the wreckage.

"Bastien! Over here!" It has to be Bastien. "You can make it!" My voice is scratchy and hoarse, I sound like some kind of wounded wild animal. Our raft rises on a big swell and then sinks into the trough. The next wave breaks, covering us. The next one raises us. The swimmer's a little closer. His arms are still moving, but I can tell he's tired. He's lost. He's so close, but he doesn't see me. He doesn't hear me even though I'm waving and screaming his name. A wave covers his head and now I don't see him. I wait for his head to reappear but it doesn't.

"Bastien!" I yell his name with all my might.

He's close, so close. I can't let him drown, I have to help him. I have to do this. Letting go of the mast and trusting the knot, my very own knot, I plunge into the sea as far as the rope will let me. Stretch out my body, my arms, reaching for him. I'm a human pole, a rope, a life buoy. Open my eyes underwater, looking for him. Around me, the dolphins slip past. I see their pink underbellies, I feel their powerful bodies against my thighs. I hear their chatters and squeaks, they're urging us not to give up. But I don't see Bastien.

Another wave covers me. I hold my breath until my lungs want to pop. The dolphins are lifting him up, bringing him to me. I'm stretching out my arm as far as I can, fanning my fingers wide. And then I feel his hand grab mine like a fish on the line. I squeeze back to let him know I've got him and wait for the wave to pass over.

At the surface I'm sucking air, I can't get enough. Bastien's crawling up on me, he's desperate to breathe. I'm reaching for the rope, pulling on it with my free hand with all my might, pulling us close to the mast, the life-saving tree trunk of a mast that Bastien cut down. I'm reaching up, trying to get my arm over the log.

"The mast!" I yell. "Grab the mast!"

His eyes are filled with panic, he doesn't seem to hear me—the explosion must've deafened him. But he sees the mast and grabs it. He clings to it, panting, choking and puking up sea water. Cutting the masthead pennant free, I take the end of the halyard and tie a bowline around his waist, securing him to the mast with the rest of us. He throws his long leg up and pulls himself onto the floating sail, pauses for breath, and then reaches down to give me a hand.

⚜

Around us, the remains of our own *Good Fortune*, scattered like charred bones in a graveyard ravaged by wild dogs. The ghost fleet is gone. Vanished. Returned to the ocean floor, leaving a cloud of hazy smoke that lingers just above the water.

It's nearly dawn. The moon is gone, the sky is a rosy gray. I can't feel my feet or my legs. My hands look like two dead starfish—wrinkled, bloated, and blue. Next to me Ming sleeps. They all sleep, huddled together. Once again I count heads to reassure myself. Once again I count seven. We're all here, side by side, huddling together for warmth. All of us, alive! But I feel another presence. There are eight of us clinging to the mast.

Yu, he's next to me, sucking the heat from my body. But he's very weak, his power nearly gone. Turning my head, I can see him in the moonlight, dressed in yellow silk, his hair in a topknot, his eyebrows and eyelashes rimed with salt crystals like frozen tears. *I'll never forget, Yu. I'll carry your memories with me all of my days. If only we could have lived at the same time, I would have been your friend.*

The dolphins are still circling us, they're cheering us on. Mazu has called them, they'll lead our rescuers to us. The ship is close now. I can feel the energy of its engines pulsating through the water, in my mind's eye I can see the steel bow cutting through the swell under the competent hands of the helmsman. *Hold on! Don't give up! Help is on the way!*

The bloated moon is low in the sky, it's turning from white to orange as it sinks into the waves. The night of the Hungry Ghost, nearly over. We've passed the place in the ocean where the dead ones went down. They have no power over us here. The dead men no longer sing in my head. Yu is fading fast;, I can't bring myself to look at him anymore. He'll vanish like a dewdrop in the morning sun. I'm sorry it has to be one or the other: Yu or me. But if it has to be, then I want to live. It's my turn. I will live.

ABOUT THE AUTHOR

Born in Baltimore, Maryland, Linda loves to travel by land, air, and sea. Her nautical stories are in part inspired by her sailing experiences, which include three weeks as a crew member aboard the HM Bark *Endeavour,* a replica of Captain Cook's renowned ship. Linda has also sailed thousands of nautical miles with her husband, Bob Russell, aboard their thirty-six-foot sloop, *Topaz.* She worked for over a decade as a registered nurse in emergency, critical care, and inpatient psychiatric care.

www.lindacollison.com

ABOUT OLD SALT PRESS

Old Salt Press is an independent press catering to those who love books about ships and the sea. We are an association of writers working together to produce the very best of nautical and maritime fiction and nonfiction. We invite you to join us as we go down to the sea in books.

www.oldsaltpress.com

Go Down to the Sea in Books with
Old Salt Press

THE SHANTYMAN
by Rick Spilman

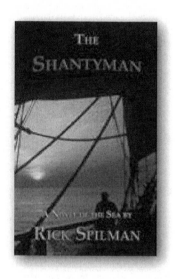

He can save the ship and the crew, but can he save himself?

In 1870, on the clipper ship *Alhambra* in Sydney, with a dying captain and a murderous mate, Jack Barlow, the shantyman, will literally keep the crew pulling together. As he struggles with a tragic past, a troubled present, and an uncertain future, Barlow will guide the *Alhambra* through Southern Ocean ice and the horror of an Atlantic hurricane. His one goal is bringing the ship and crew safely back to New York, where he hopes to start anew. Based on a true story, **The Shantyman** is a gripping tale of survival against all odds at sea and ashore and the challenge of facing a past that can never be wholly left behind.

ISBN 978-0994115232

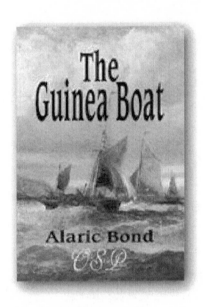

Alaric Bond's eighth novel, **The Guinea Boat**. Set in Hastings, Sussex, during the early part of 1803, **The Guinea Boat** tells the story of two young lads and the diverse paths they take to make a living on the water. Britain is still at an uneasy peace with France, but there is action and intrigue aplenty along the southeast coast. Private fights and family feuds abound; a hot press threatens the livelihoods of many, while the newly re-formed Sea Fencibles begin a careful watch on Bonaparte's ever-growing invasion fleet. And to top it all, free trading has grown to the extent that it is now a major industry, and one barely kept in check by the efforts of the preventive men.

ISBN 978-0994115294

Go Down to the Sea in Books with
Old Salt Press

BRITANNIA'S SHARK
by Antione Vanner

Britannia's Shark is the third of the Dawlish Chronicles novels. It's 1881 and a daring act of piracy draws the ambitious British naval officer Nicholas Dawlish into a deadly maelstrom of intrigue and revolution. Drawn in too is his wife, Florence, for whom the glimpse of a half-forgotten face evokes memories of earlier tragedy.

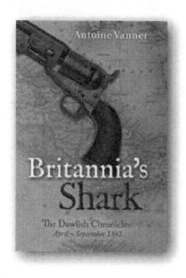

For a nightmare lies ahead, amid both the wealth and squalor of America's Gilded Age and on a fever-ridden island ruled by savage tyranny. Manipulated ruthlessly from London by the shadowy Admiral Topcliffe, Nicholas and Florence Dawlish must make some very strange alliances if they are to survive—and prevail.

ISBN 978-0992263690

Go Down to the Sea in Books with
Old Salt Press

ELEANOR'S ODYSSEY
by Joan Druett

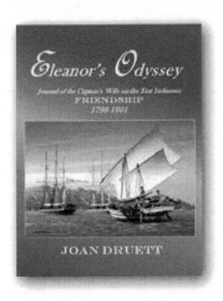

It was 1799, and French privateers lurked in the Atlantic and the Bay of Bengal. Yet Eleanor Reid, newly married and just twenty-one years old, made up her mind to sail with her husband, Captain Hugh Reid, to the penal colony of New South Wales, the Spice Islands, and India. Danger threatened not just from the barely charted seas they would be sailing; yet, confident in her love and her husband's seamanship, Eleanor insisted on going along. Joan Druett, writer of many books about the sea, including the best seller *Island of the Lost* and the groundbreaking story of women under sail, *Hen Frigates*, embellishes Eleanor's journal with a commentary that illuminates the strange story of a remarkable young woman.

ISBN 978-0-9941152-1-8

Go Down to the Sea in Books with
Old Salt Press

BLACKWELL'S HOMECOMING

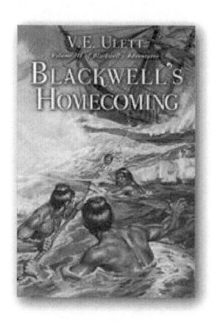

by V. E. Ulett

Volume III of the *Blackwell's Adventures* Series

In a multigenerational saga of love, war, and betrayal, Captain Blackwell and Mercedes continue their voyage in Volume III of ***Blackwell's Adventures***. The Blackwell family's eventful journey from England to Hawaii, by way of the new and tempestuous nations of Brazil and Chile, provides an intimate portrait of family conflicts and loyalties in the late Georgian Age. ***Blackwell's Homecoming*** is an evocation of the dangers and rewards of desire.
ISBN 978-0-9882360-7-3

Made in the USA
San Bernardino, CA
29 May 2015